SWALLOWS ALSO FALL

CR ARMENY

BlueRose ONE .com
Stories Matter

BLUEROSE PUBLISHERS UK Ltd.
London

This book is primarily published and distributed in Great Britain and is also available in other global marketplaces.

BlueRose ONE.com
Stories Matter

ISBN: 978-93-7139-007-1

Designed and distributed by **BlueRoseONE.com** with global reach. Printing and fulfilment are managed through international distribution networks, ensuring availability based on order locations.

For publishing inquiries, visit **www.BlueRoseONE.com**

BlueRose Publishers UK Ltd,
Unit 3, 6-7 St Mary at Hill, London

+44 7386286323

First Edition: July 2025

Novel extract from Swallows also Fall

Marcel-lí Massana was a resistant fighter after the Spanish Civil War. The story is told from the point of view of a foster sister Rosana. He was forced to go to the city of Solsona to study to become a priest like his uncle. Marcel-lí was rebellious and didn't want to have anything with religion. At the age of seventeen, he volunteered to fight for the Republic. After the war, he was a prisoner in a concentration camp and later in prison. After the war, he founded a resistance group known as the Maqui.

Chapter 1

Autumn 1944

Autumn was dry. And up in the small village of El Pont; the Tramontana wind lasted almost a week. The wind blew hard, raking dead leaves that tumbled along and ended in the ditch. Days went by without the shadow of a cloud scudding over the grey mountains—no sparrows flew over the neighbouring orchards. And to our chagrin, instead of edible mushrooms, only poisonous toadstools grew in the local pine forest. Our village received the most harrowing piece of news since the war. It happened early one morning in the village of Vilada: A local man walking his dog found three dead men. At first, he thought that he saw a bundle of old clothes, but then he had a shock, he saw three bodies soaked in blood. The men had been shot in the head and dumped by the bridge.

My name is Rosana, and since my husband Oriól had returned from Cardona concentration camp, we lived with our daughter Nina in a house by the river Llobregat. In front of our house, the river's strong currents had washed away the soil, and a wooden bridge connected the house to the land. Oriól bought a few planks from the sawmill where he worked and built a bench and a washing line. There we would sit in winter to enjoy the warm afternoon sun and dry the washing. I put a few geranium pots on one side and in the summertime, our black cat sprawled out under the cool shade of the geraniums. In winter he enjoyed sleeping over the sun-warmed banister.

On the other side of the river, there was a small grey train station. There was only one passenger train a day, the other trains carried coal from the Figuls' mines to the city of Barcelona. A wooden footbridge had been built on stilts for passengers to cross to our side. I was afraid of crossing it myself because the poles shook with the current and the planks trembled under my footsteps.

Whoever, I enjoyed looking at people crossing the bridge because you only saw part of their bodies, and you could hear the children laughing without seeing them. They emerged at the end of the bridge in front of our house.

I wasn't going to worry my daughter Nina about the news when she got back home from school. However, when Oriól returned, he blurted out the whole story. The men were Maquis, and no one had any doubts: Franco's Civil Guard had executed them.

"What's going to happen to us? Nina asked.

"Well, nothing. People here don't know that we're related to the Maquis," Oriól said.

I crossed myself.

"Why were they shot?" Nina looked confused.

"According to the authorities, the Civil Guard shot them while they were trying to escape arrest."

I couldn't move, I couldn't think I only crossed myself. The day I feared so much had arrived. My head spun with all kinds of thoughts. I went into the kitchen to drink water and did the dishes and cried. Oriól became very irritated when he saw tears, and he also hated prayers. He called himself an atheist and was contemptuous of any form of religion. He would say that people of faith saw themselves as if they were the only possessors of the absolute truth and the rest 'the possessors of pure bullshit'."

I waited for him and Nina to go to bed, and when they were fast asleep, I felt free to pray and cry. The next morning to our horror, six coaches full of Civil Guards arrived in the town of Berga. They lodged in the army's quarters dressed in dark-green uniforms, the majority sported black bushy moustaches that hid their rotten teeth and cruel smiles. Their heavy boots creaked as they walked in pairs up and down the main street loaded with guns. Sometimes, they turned up into the city's intricate alleyways like stray dogs.

Shortly after lunch, I went to hang out a couple of kitchen towels. I heard the whistle of the train approaching. Then the usual screech of the rusty breaks. After a few seconds, the train's engine puffed with new energy and a trail of thick, black smoke blurred the view. The wooden train swayed noisily, and it disappeared down the river's gorge. And my God! What a fright! I saw two figures dressed in reptilian-green uniforms with black, patent-leather hats. The pair of Civil Guards began crossing the bridge. They approached stomping like horses on the wooden bridge. I didn't see anyone else, only the ghostly guards with the ugly, ancient and menacing hats.

Oh dear, I was going to die in that spot. My head spun, my mouth went dry and then a chill ran all over my body. My first thought was to hide from them. Still holding a towel in my hand, I rushed into the house and carefully closed the door. I watched the sinister guards from behind the window nets wondering with what intention they were coming to our home. I bit the towel hard as not to bite my finger, but the guards plodded up the hill without a look at our house. I wondered where they could be going.

In the evening, Oriól said that the guards were only making inquiries and exploring the area. They came from other parts of the country and didn't know the local geography. But I was sure the guards had come to kill the resistance fighters. That night I knew perfectly well how people condemned to death felt. Memories of their childhood passed like shadows in their tortured minds as if they could live their life again.

Chapter 2

Castellar del Riu Year 1918

When Baby Marcel-lí arrived at our house he was so sick that Mother didn't believe that he would live much longer. In those days, we lived as tenant farmers in a hamlet with only three scattered farmhouses and a little church on the other side of a valley. Father said that France was only about eight hours walking away, but only smugglers knew the paths. To the left, the land dropped down the river Aigua D'Ora, and there was the village of Llinas with only a few scatted houses a church, an inn and a school for boys. There was not enough money for another school, so the girls stayed home. Beyond the valley was a bare mountain pass called Port de Compte. On the right, there was the river Aiguas de Llinas and the giant Busa Mountain Range.

I remember that the swallows had flown away, the bees were in their hives and the insects that hadn't died in the cold sheltered under the bark of trees. In the evening, as we gathered around the fire, the forest became alive with the sharp screeching of the barn owl, the ghostly "ooh-hu, ooh-hu, ooh-hu!" of the eagle owl, and at times, the terrifying howling of wolves.

Our Father was the only person who could read and write in the village. Sometimes, Father and the landlord would talk about things that happened in faraway places such as Madrid. The word sounded strange, but in that place, there was a palace with the king and his ministers. From what I heard Father telling the landlord, I imagined that the palace was a big house full of well-dressed people running around like scared ants, but never getting any work done.

Late in the afternoon, I would come out to call the chickens home before the fox grabbed one of them. I used to hit an aluminium dish of sweet corn with a wooden spoon, and it was great fun to see them running fast to be the first to feed on the corn. They had been wandering around digging for worms, but chickens were always hungry. The black cockerel was the first and the old red hen the last, so I kept some corn in my hand for her. After locking the coop, I saw that Father and the landlord had stopped loading dry alfalfa from a cart into the shed. The landlord leaned his stocky body on a pitchfork. His face was round, red and a deep line crossed his broad forehead. The man was a little short of hearing, and when Father talked to him, he gazed straight into his eyes, and it gave me the impression that he was trying to listen with his eyes. I never said anything about it for fear that Josep would laugh at me.

Father started talking about the flu.

"A real killer," he said.

"God help us," the landlord moved the fork to his left hand and crossed himself.

I didn't know whether I had to cross myself or not.

"Is it that bad?" The landlord asked.

"Oh, yes. I read it in the paper," Father added, "worse than the plague," his hand fumbled in his pocket.

I sat at the edge of the drinking trough.

Father got out his smoking paper and then the tobacco pouch. He started to roll a cigarette when a gust of wind tore the paper away from his fingers, and it fell onto a dunghill.

"Ouch!" He grimaced, "It's a real tragedy," and he got out another paper. The landlord pursed his lips, and the line between his eyes got deeper.

"Well, but we can pray."

"Oh yes, and we do pray," Father said and looked away.

I went indoors.

The following Sunday after lunch, Mother was clearing the rabbit bones from our plates and making a neat pile. My twelve-year-old brother Josep sat next to Father, and I sat next to Mother to help. I think that I was about ten. Ernest was four, and he was sitting next to Josep, and baby Ramón sat on Father's lap. I believed that Mother was going to take the pile of plates to the kitchen, but she said.

"I'm going to nurse a new baby."

Ramón knocked on the table; his bowl fell on the floor, and before I had time to pick up the pieces, the dogs began to bark. Father got up and stepped down into the entrance hall that served as a kitchen.

"Good afternoon! A male voice echoed in the house.

"Oh, they're here already!" Mother said.

A tall man and a woman carrying a well wrapped up baby came into the dining room.

"My name is Manel, and this is my sister Pepeta," he said.

"Come in," Father said.

I couldn't move my eyes from Pepeta's face. The dogs stopped barking, and we all fell silent. It was as if we were afraid of breathing. All eyes were fixed on each slow movement of Pepeta's arms as she placed the baby in Mother's arms. Once the baby was safe, Pepeta sobbed. Josep and Ernest remained seated and looked as if they all had indigestion, but Ramón was angry and kicked Father. Mother went into her room, and Pepeta followed her. The baby cried and then fell silent and cried again. Father offered Manel Mother's chair.

"From the river to here it's a long pull up the hill," Father said.

"It is indeed," Manel panted. Father passed him the wine porró. Manel rose the porró, opened his mouth and gulped down the wine that spurted from the spout. Josep was checking his hair parting with his hand and flattening it down. Ernest was picking his nose, and I gave him a little nudge before Father saw him. Manel stopped drinking, wiped a drop of wine off his chin and then laid the porró back on the table. I finished picking up the pieces of the broken bowl and took them to the ash bucket in the kitchen. I glanced at Manel, his new, black corduroy trousers were very black and his new white shirt very white. He was younger and healthier than the farmers I used to see. Next to him, Father's blue shirt looked sad and faded for having spent so much time in the sun. He rolled out another cigarette and offered his tobacco pouch to Manel.

"I don't smoke thanks," he said.

Father took a few puffs on his cigarette and said.

"I heard that things' are not going well in the town?" he asked.

Manel nodded. I peeped into Mother's room, and she was sitting on her bed, trying to breastfeed the puny baby. I felt I was losing my Mother.

"We'd been feeding him rice water," Pepeta said.

"Rice water is good," Mother added as she tried to encourage the baby to

suck a little more.

In the dining room, the talk continued.

"The city is awash with grief," Manel said; "as soon as St John's bell begins to toll for the dead, St Peter's bell starts as well. And before they stop St

Francis's bell joins in. The ringing never stops, as soon as one ringing ends, another begins. It's a nightmare."

"Rosana bring the hot water we had heated for the washing up." Mother called from the room. I got up and went down to the kitchen. I poured the hot water from the pan hanging from the crook over the fire into a bucket, tested that it wasn't too hot and carried it into the bedroom. She began to take the baby's clothes off. The baby opened his eyes, and I saw two, sad blue stars. This baby wasn't like us because we had dark eyes.

"He's so thin," Mother said, lifting the baby's legs cleaning his red bottom.

"We were afraid of feeding him cow's milk because they say it's too strong."

I rushed to pick the smelly nappy from the floor and took it out of the house, to the outside washing-tub let the water wash away the runny poo. Then, I sat listening to our Father and Manel.

"It is heart-breaking, women and children in black," Manel said.

Mother and Pepeta went out to wash their hands.

"You must eat something," Mother said.

"We must leave before it gets dark," Pepeta said.

"Many, many thanks for your help," Manel added as they began to walk out of

the house. Father accompanied him with baby Ramón in his arms. We always did when someone visited. Josep, Ernest and I followed as well. We walked in silence in a single file in front of the farmyard and down the thorn, hedged winding path that separated the terraced fields from the forest. A long-tailed lizard scuttled into a prickly bush. We stopped at the edge of the pine forest. I loved the smell of resin, oozing out from pine trees. Marcel-lí's Father looked at us, and we shook hands.

"We'll pray for the baby and the mother," Father said. Manel stroked baby Ramón's hair said goodbye. Pepeta cried, and both walked down towards the river. A startled magpie screeched and flew over the forest canopy. As we walked back, a gust of cold wind hit my bare legs, and I shivered. Baby Ramón was asleep in Father's arms.

Back in the house, Father left Ramón in the cradle while Ernest and I rushed into the room to see the new baby. Josep stood at the door and asked.

"Has he got the flu?"

"Good God! I hope not," Mother sighed.

Father went to feed the animals, and Josep followed him. Ernest returned to the hall to play with the toy train that Josep had made for him by stringing together empty sardine tins that road workers had thrown away. He began to pull, and the train moved from side to side like a giant caterpillar imitating the sound of the steam. Choo-choo-choo. He went around the house.

"Now that both babies are asleep, we'll start getting the vegetables ready for supper."

Mother picked a basket of potatoes and sat down to peel them. I picked out the small ones; when we finished, she washed them, filled a pan with water and hung it over the fire.

"Ernest," Mother called. "Bring some firewood."

Ernest fetched a few sticks from a pile in the corner by the front door and left them next to Mother. She broke them with her hands, the twigs creaked and one by one she put them into the fire. An instant blaze followed; the small, dry leaves burned into small flames that lived only for a few seconds. The fireplace glowed and felt warm and cosy. Then we heard the faint cry of the new baby.

"Quick girl hold him! Before he falls out of bed," Mother said.

I picked up the baby afraid that the frail baby might slip out of my hands. Ramón woke up screaming.

"Don't take any notice."

How could I not take notice? I rushed to Ramón with one baby in my arms and tried to calm him with the other. Mother pushed the pan to one side and cooked a small pot of semolina for Ramón. I fed him the semolina and Mother feed Marcel-lí. At dusk, I was exhausted.

The landlord's house was the biggest in the hamlet. It was three floors high with a balcony and several windows and a little church on the side. Our home was a cottage standing in front of the landlord's house right at the edge of the hill. From the house, we could see the church Our Lady of 'La Mata.' on the other side of the valley. The story says that when Muslims had invaded the country, they destroyed religious icons. Then people hid religious paintings and sculptures in the forest. Later, a local cowherd found the image Our Lady inside a box shrub, and it was called our lady of La Mata.

Our cottage was a simple home with an entrance hall that served as a kitchen. A good fire was indispensable; winters were harsh, wet and windy. Our fireplace had a wall to keep us warm. The kitchen had a table for Mother to make cheese, and then she left to rest for a few days inside a warm cupboard with star-shaped holes on both doors. There was a sink made of stone by the window. Behind the kitchen, there was a small room with an oven to bake bread, and at the end of the dark corridor, there was the wooden toiled. The dining room and bedrooms were at the back of the house, facing the deep valley down below and the Busar hills. In the evening, we sat around the fire to say the family rosary. Father had learned the whole prayer by heart and holding the rosary in his hand, recited the first mystery. We responded in a chorus of Hail Marys. I wasn't smart enough to understand the healing beauty of the prayer. I got bored, and to keep awake I sat at the back, next to a flickering candle, and I amused myself collecting the falling drops of wax on my fingernails and waiting until they dried and then peeled them off one by one.

The devil lived in a cranny behind the toilet. He was skulking there until one of us misbehaved, and then he would come to our room in the middle of the night and drag us away by our feet. I never saw him but, I could hear him breathing when I went there late at night to pee. So, I waited till someone else needed to go and follow them and then ran as quickly as I could. Sometimes, it felt safer to go out and pee on the grass by the cliff. In my sleep, I tried to keep my legs curled up high to my neck so that in the darkness, the devil wouldn't be able to find them.

That night I didn't dream of the devil but the flu. In the town, the funerary cart's driver was so exhausted that he lost his mind and drove the horses along the streets grabbing anyone he found on his way and throwing them into the cart regardless of whether they were dead or alive.

Chapter 3

"Kikiriduuuu!" The black cockerel crowed, "Kikiriduuuu!" The landlord's cockerel also crowed and one by one the cockerels from other farms followed like a song. I was glad to see the light of day. Outside, the valley was still green, but a heavy snowfall had turned the distant hills into beautiful, white graves. I got dressed to the clang of iron handles hitting zinc buckets of swill and a racket of squealing pigs. Father had started his work on the farm. I was washing my face when Ramón began to yell, and the bitter smell of burning reached from the kitchen. As I picked Ramón up, Marcel-lí began to cry. I carried Ramón to the kitchen, and Mother was bending over a pot of semolina.

"Good morning, Mother," I said, but no reply.

"We've got a lot to do."

The babies smelled of fresh poo, and with tired eyes, she moved the pot to one side. Mother changed Ramón's nappy and washed his face. I wiped baby Marcel-lí, fearful that my fingers might break his delicate skin. Having finished, I took out the soiled nappies. The sun was rising, the church's bells were ringing for prayer, and I prayed the Matins. The hens had seen me, and they began to move around impatiently, waiting for their freedom. I opened the coop, and a rush of colourful hens followed. They ran and ran clacking, flapping to the meadow.

Back to the house, Mother was holding Marcel-lí to her breast with one hand and spooning semolina into Ramón's mouth with the other. There was no fry-up for breakfast, but we had milk. Josep came down, patting his wet hair with his right hand, he drank a glass of milk and left for school munching a chunk of bread. With sleep in his eyes, Ernest came down to the kitchen. The boy needed a wash. After gulping a glass of milk, he looked around.

"Where's my train? He asked.

"Where did you leave it last night?" Mother asked.

"I found it! I found it! Under the bench."

While he pulled his train around the house, Mother went out to fetch water from the spring.

"Mmmmm," Ramón kicked and babbled.

My God! What struggle it was to sweep the floor. The broom's handle was too long and got stuck on the table's crossed legs. It made me very angry because I couldn't reach bits of dry soil from Father's espadrilles on the floor. Ramón was trying to crawl and climb the bench. I pulled him away but he fell on the floor crying. Mother returned to the house with a bucket of water from the spring and poured it into a cooking pot and hung it on the crook. She made a fire she added a few pork bones, and a dumpling made with the fat of a hen.

"Don't let the fire die out," she said as she peeled potatoes for the pot.

I sat with both babies by the fire and when the flames fizzled out, I added twigs and fanned the coals. The fire flared up, the pot boiled over and shit! The fire went dead. Only a nest of black coals and wet ash was left.

"Girl, how many times do I have to tell you, you must feed the fire slowly. Look, look at this mess."

I felt ashamed of my clumsiness. Mother removed the wet coals and built a new fire. By one o'clock I lay the table, I put the porró on one side and a plate with sliced bread on the other. Father came home, picked up Ramón from the floor, washed his hands in a bowl of water and sat at the table with him on his lap. Mother brought the steaming soup in a bone-white tureen and placed it at the centre of the table. Father lifted the lid, and a delicious cloud of steam came out of the chipped tureen. Father served himself very carefully, and Mother served the children. After lunch, Father got back to work, Mother and I did the washing up. Then we went out to wash the nappies, and I hang them on the thorn hedge to dry them in the sun.

Mother went back to check on the babies, and I stood there, letting my eyes wander at the row of perfect ridges folding one into the other. The ridges ended abruptly in a flat top. The beautiful mountain range had a sad history. During the French invasion, the flat top had been used as a prison; prisoners were led to the top, where they were forced to traverse a chasm that separated the flat top and the other side of the mountain on a plank of wood. The plank would be removed, and the unfortunate souls were left to die. The prisoners jumped into the chasm below, screaming, 'Die in Busa and rise again in Paris.' At the bottom of the cliff, a pack of hungry wolves was waiting for them. I couldn't imagine what kind of crime they could have committed. The word Paris had a lovely sound. I thought that Paris must be a beautiful place to live and Busa a horrible place to die.

"I found mushrooms," Josep crowed imitating cockerels. It was time for me to get back into the house. Josep ate bread with jam and went to help Father who had to clean the landlord's pigsty. Ernest pulled his train around the dining room table. Mother and I peeled the potatoes and put them to cook. Cleaning the mushroom was a real joy. I loved the soft and humid surface, rubbing my fingers over the odd and beautiful shape and pulling out the bits of dead grass that sometimes got stuck on them. Then cut off the knobby roots and scraped the soil from the stalks, washed them and fried them.

After supper, we sat to hull the sweet corn. It was a time full of surprise as we peeled off the cob's dry leaves, sometimes a beautiful ruby-red or black cob would emerge. It was a moment of great joy as the special cobs were the most beautiful thing that I had ever seen.

Our little joy vanished the following afternoon with the mad barking of dogs. Father Gerard's black cassock had scared them. Marcel-lí woke up crying. Father left the landlord's cows' shed, washed his hands and came to welcome the priest.

"Sad news for you," Father Gerard said. "The baby's mother has died."

Mother closed her eyes as if in intense pain, then she crossed herself, and I did the same.

"It's God's will," he added.

"Yes," Father said. Mother picked up Marcel-lí from the cradle and brought him for the priest while Ernest held his train close to his heart.

"Oh, he looks better," Father Gerard said.

“He had been sick with diarrhoea,” Mother said.

"It's normal in small babies. It's going to be a great consolation for his family."

Marcel-lí's eyes were closing, and Mother put him back.

The priest had a drink of wine and left with Father.

Mother picked up a basket of clothes that needed mending. I sat tearful Ramón on a blanket on the floor, and Mother picked up her sewing and gave me a sock with a small hole on the heel. She put a wooden egg inside to stretch it, threaded the needle and put the needle in my fingers and said.

"Be careful not to prick your finger and don't make it too tight, or it will look like a hen's bottom."

Holding the sock and the egg and pushing the needle at the same time was a struggle. My hand wasn't big enough to hold the egg; it slipped out of my hand, and I pricked myself. I screamed.

"Let it bleed," Mother said, "it will heal by itself." Josep arrived. His face was flushed and sweaty from walking uphill. I told him that father Gerard had been to the house and Josep said.

"Did he come to bring us the flu or to rip his cassock?"

"He said nothing about his cassock, Marcel-lí's Mother has died," Mother added.

"Oh, I'm sorry," Josep said, and he crossed himself. What's going to happen to the baby now?" He asked.

Mother stopped her sewing.

"We just don't know," she signed with the idle sewing needle between her fat fingers.

Chapter 4

Oh dear, the sky was darkening fast, and the nappies are outside. I went out to pick them up. I walked past the washing tub and the hens' house. A single star twinkled above the snow-white Port de Compte, and nothing stirred in the valley down below. A thick winter mist was falling, but a few shreds slithered over the snow-white mountain range. But as I stood there gaping at the wonders of grey mist swirling over the snow.

"ZZZZZup!" An orange-eyed monster dashed over my head. What a fright! I nearly fell to the ground. The desperate squeals of a mouse being swallowed up alive followed, my body trembled, my head spun, and I could hear my heart beating in my fingertips. With quick, jerky movements, I pulled the nappies one by one dumped them into the basket and tried to rush home but with a basket in my hands. I couldn't run. I only hobbled to the house feeling trapped like the mouse.

Mother had exchanged the needle for a knife, and she sat by fire peeling potatoes. Josep was stoking the fire, and Ernest small hand was cradling Marcel-lí. Ramón sat on a blanket chewing at one end.

"The Catalan Commonwealth have planned a telephone system," Josep said, as his fingers tried to roll a cigarette.

"What for," Mother asked.

"To call the doctor," Josep said.

"The flu is killing hundreds of people every day, and what can doctors do about it?"

"Sign the death certificate, urgently," he laughed.

"Bah! Comforts for the rich," Mother added. "See what the doctors could do for poor Marcel-lí's mother."

At the weekend, when Marcel-lí's Father arrived, he handed out a few sweets, but his time they were bitter lemon candy. Father rushed to shake hands and expressed his condolence. Then he picked up the baby, and while holding him close to his chest, he began to talk about the flu.

"People are stricken suddenly; a blue tint appears in their faces, soon they collapse in the street coughing up blood and die a few hours later." Mother moved her head sideways. Father pursed his lips, and Josep put his hand over his hair parting. Ernest's fingers grabbed Mother's skirt. I listened, gripped by horror.

"With so many dead, one cannot stop thinking that the end of the world is here," Father said.

"It feels like it," Marcel-lí's Father said. "Children are no longer allowed to come out and play in the streets."

"So distressing," Father said.

Bells were ringing, people turning blue people falling—life had gone topsy-turvy.

In the night, I curled up under the blankets and felt safe. But not for long something heave stirred under my window. It was grunting and rooting around. I recalled what Mother used to say. Girl, it's only a boar.

The boars ate our crops. They loved sweetcorn and farmers shot them and shared the meat with the rest of the villagers. The problem was that no one knew when the boars would turn up. It was a long time since the landlord killed a boar. We made boar sausages and preserved them in clay pots covered in lard.

At last, Father and the landlord had finished the task of putting dry grass stored in the barn before the snow fell. Wet hay rots inside the barn. The winter sun no longer dried the daily load of nappies, and we hang them on a cane over the hearth. I had chilblains in my fingers and toes. The woolly winter socks would not keep out the cold from my feet, and in the warmth of the bed, the chilblains came to life and itched. Mother told me to rub them with raw garlic. But I hated the smell of garlic in my bed, so I had to scratch my toes for some time before falling asleep.

Baby Marcel-lí was dreaming with the angels because he was smiling in his sleep. We were very proud of the blue-eyed baby that we had looked after so carefully. Ramón was already walking around. He had learned to throw things away, and he enjoyed practising all day. It got dark at five o'clock in the afternoon that meant that Christmas was approaching. The sky had remained bright and clear, but late in the afternoon, a red and ugly patch appeared behind the Busa Mountain range. It was a bad omen. The next day, a horrid Tramontana wind began to blow. First, I saw a few leaves blowing over the roof then hitting the door. The wind gathered strength, and soon the oak tree was bare. Then it roared around the house and got in through cracks on the roof and whistled as it filtered under the doors.

"God, this house shakes as if possessed by a bad spirit," Mother said, and she rushed to shut the windows. The wind whistled through every corner, and it came down the chimney. The fire went out.

"This wind makes people ill," Mother said.

We heard a roof tile falling to the ground together with the rock that Father had placed on it. Josep did not return from school that evening. He stayed in our uncle's mill by the river. I was glad of the wind because it scared away the animals that roamed around in the night making scary sounds.

The flu came by boat from America. Father said, and the wretched thing was so infectious that the authorities distributed free bleach to the poor and taking flowers to the cemetery was banned.

Chapter 5

"What drama is Christmas Eve!" Mother said, hanging a pot of water on the crook over the fire. Then she went to the backroom and came back with a dish full of sweet corn.

"Let's go and catch him," she said as she took the kitchen knife and went out. She stood on the threshing floor, hitting the pot with the wooden spoon, scattering handfuls of corn on the ground and calling "co, co, co, co, co, co!" Hens and young chickens of all colours came from all directions to feast on the corn. The black cockerel with his beautiful red crest and curving black tail came running to his death. Mother grabbed him by his wings, and with a knife cut under the cockerel's ear, blood began to flow on the dish. The cockerel struggled to break free, and I watched its eyelids closing slowly and slowly, his legs becoming weaker and weaker the struggle was over. Mother dipped the cockerel into the boiling water, and we began to pluck the bird.

After supper, Father and Josep placed a big log by the hearth. It had to be kept warm through the night; otherwise, the magic won't work. Later, instead of going to bed, Father, Josep, and the landlord walked for the midnight mass known as the cockerel mass. 'La Misa De Gall'.

On Christmas morning, the silence made me feel as if I were in a different world. No cockerels crewing and the view from the window was white, pure and clean. The old barnyard's roof was a white field, the fence a white line and the church was hardly visible. Snow is so white so radiant, but so cold. Despite the cold, I felt that the day ahead was going to be very special. After the daily chores, we all gathered around the hearth. The log was burning at one end. Ernest picked up a stick and began to hit the wood, Josep laughed. He was too old to believe in such nonsense as the "Shitting Log." We had to watch Ramón because he was tottering about and could fall on the fire. Mother gave him a stick and sang.

"Log, log, shit sweets otherwise I hit you with the stick."

Ernest's joyful voice was the loudest, but Ramón babbled, and Ernest helped him and together they played the game.

Ernest lifted the blanket, and he found sweets, torró and a bottle of brandy for Father.

"Look! What I found," he said. I took the torró in my hand, and admired the colourful cover, wondering what it meant. I traced each letter with my finger pretending that I wrote it myself. Father was laughing because Ramón tried to eat the sweet with the wrapping paper.

"No, no silly boy!" Ernest said, removing the wrapping from the sweet for him.

Lunch consisted of a special soup made with chicken giblets, ham bone, and vegetables boiled together for a long time, delicious. For the main course, we had the cockerel cooked in a casserole with wild mushrooms and brandy. For dessert, we had Torró. It was a real treat.

A few days later, Father read that in Barcelona, they had run out of coffins to bury the dead. In the 'Good Shepherd's poor house, flu victims were taken to the cemetery at the back of trucks and dumped into mass graves. It was a pitiful end. I thought that perhaps in the city, there was no guardian angel.

A harness broke, and the landlord went to town to buy a new one, and on his return, he called into our house. It was late, Mother was peeling potatoes, Josep was doing his homework, Father was sharpening a knife, and my little brother Ernest was pulling his train around. I sat with baby Marcel-lí on my lap while Ramón was on the floor playing with an old blanket.

"I must warn you about something that has happened in the village of El Pont," he said.

Mother stopped peeling the potatoes, and the landlord looked around.

"It's about the devil," he said.

"Did you say the devil?" Father asked and left the knife on the table.

"Yes, he appeared at an inn," the landlord said, "it was late in the evening." A

"You mean in human form?"

"Yes," the landlord nodded.

Ernest left his train, and Josep gapped.

"The innkeeper became suspicious of a man wearing a smart raincoat and patent leather, black shoes."

"Such a well-dressed person has never done an honest day's work," Father added.

"When the innkeeper told him, it was time to close the bar; the devil did not reply. After a while, the innkeeper asked again and no reply. Then the innkeeper looked more closely and saw two little horns half-hidden in the man's curly hair. Horrified, he ran to call the priest."

"Call the priest at that time?" Father asked.

"Yes, the priest got up from his bed, put on his cassock, grabbed a bible and the cross and rushed to the inn with no other clothes except an undone cassock," the landlord snarled, and a giggle escaped from my mouth.

"The devil growls," the landlord said.

"Like a wolf in a trap," Mother added.

"That's right he twisted and turned and was so mad at the sight of the cross that he didn't know which way to run. The priest began to say a special prayer, and the devil, limped to the door. His shoes didn't fit his animal's hooves."

Ernest was cowering in Mother's skirts, and Marcel-lí started kicking. I picked him up, but my sympathy was for the poor devil. I couldn't run because I had chilblains, but the devil couldn't run because his shoes were too elegant for him. How sad.

"Thank God the village had a priest. If it had happened to us, here: we wouldn't have known what to do," Mother said.

"I don't think the devil would come here," reassured the landlord, "he had some business in that place."

"The devil doesn't waste his time," Father added.

The landlord crossed himself and said.

"God bless our hamlet." And he walked out of the door. The rest of us huddled together next to Father. I was desperate to pee, but I was terrified of meeting the devil along the corridor. I couldn't hold it any longer, so I slipped out of the house and peed by the front door.

After supper, Mother fed Marcel-lí, and I washed the dishes for the first time. Father put a pan of hot water in the sink and dropped some soda crystals in the water. He brought the low chair from the fireplace and put it in front of the sink. I climbed on the chair, and I washed each dish feeling grown-up. But the feeling faded away as soon as the water got cold and felt greasy and slippery. By the time I had to wash the big cooking pot, I was bored and tired, being a grown-up was no fun. Mother must have seen it in my face because she told me to leave the pot in the water, and that she would wash it the following day. What a relief! We prayed to God to keep the devil out of our village. Before getting into bed, I looked under it, making sure No Devils were waiting for me. But I only saw a pair of old espadrilles that we kept to use in bad weather so as not to ruin the new ones. I was so tired that I fell asleep regardless of the devils roaming in the nearby villages.

The young cockerel began to crow, and soon we heard other cockerels. Getting water from the spring was harder every day. I filled the bucket to the brim, and as I walked the water splashed on my dress and espadrilles. The cold, hard bucket's handle hurt my fingers, and the mountain wind carried tiny bits of ice. I hobbled back to the house like an older woman. When I reached the house, I couldn't feel anything at all. I sat at the corner of the hearth, but the direct heat made my hands more painful. Ramón became irritable, and Marcel-lí developed the habit of kicking everything around him.

Father went from long periods of sullen silence to openly expressing anger against the harshness of country life. Mother was busy making cheese and bread. Josep tried hard to be a tough grown-up in charge of killing the rabbits. By the middle of the morning, the sun was already hot, and the snow was melting. Down below, the valley had become a beautiful pattern of green and white shapes. Ernest saw all kinds of animals in those patterns, a white horse was lying under a pine tree, and as the day went by the horse lost its legs. In the afternoon, its head had melted. In the evening, the horse had become a sleepy badger, and the world around us was all patches of black and white. During the night, the ground froze. The following morning the foottracks were dangerously hard and slippery as the morning went by the hot sun thawed the ice into slush. The younger children had to stay indoors. I was in charge of fetching fresh drinking water from the spring. Walking on snow drenched my espadrilles, and my toes felt like icicles that could break any minute.

From time to time, Josep would bring a newspaper from the inn in Llinas. He would read the paper in his usual hoity-toity manner. This time the paper didn't talk about the flu, but something called unions and strikes. In Barcelona, they found a member of the CNT union murdered in the middle of the street.

"It's a political murder," he said and looked straight at my face expecting me to ask him what a political murder was, but I didn't.

"Strikes, murders and more strikes," Mother said. "I could never go on strike. I couldn't allow the animals that feed us to die of hunger."

I only had one single thought in my mind: The spring.

Chapter 6

Spring 1922

The devil must have got buried in household dust because five years had passed, and I never met him. The flu was water under the bridge, and the boys enjoyed going to school. Josep had become moody and argumentative. Quite often, he would argue with Father because he thought that there was a colourful world beyond three farmhouses scattered on the hills. Father called me his "little woman" as I wasn't a child anymore. In our lives, the only changes come with the seasons that go from baking hot to freezing.

At the end of the month, as soon as the dogs barked the boys ran downhill to meet Marcel-lí's Father and the hill would become alive with the loud chatter of children's voices. How happy I was then to see them walking up in lively conversation, and their small hands full of sweets. That day Marcel-lí's Father brought a magazine written in Catalan. Josep was delighted, but I laughed at the city's people's clothes. Before leaving Marcel-lí's Father told us at Corpus Christi, we were going to see, "La Patum". The festival dates from the Middle Ages when the Moors invaded the town. There would be giants, winged angels, and horned devils. The young children were very excited, and they pretended to be in the middle of the festival dancing in the dining room. It was difficult to control them.

"I'm going to hit the devil with a stick," Marcel-lí said.

"I'm going to ride the eagle," Ramón replied. Mother laughed, and the boys danced for the rest of the afternoon.

In May the thorn hedge was covered in white blossom. The Goldfinch sang all day near the wildflower-spotted meadow. The hens roamed around digging, cackling and squabbling for worms. The red hen hatched a brood of chicks that ran around chirping. "piu, piu piu in frail voices." I loved to pick them up and feel their tiny hearts ticking in my hands. The soft touch of the chicks down on my face gave me shivers. Quite often, a cow would scream with labour pains, and Mother would be up all night tending the poor animal.

"We are born in pain, and we die in pain." Mother said. I shuddered.

The first swallow of the season flew around the house again.

The day before Corpus Christi, Father got up earlier than usual to feed the farm animals: The squealing of the pigs woke me up. I got up first to get the children washed, dressed and ready for the expected trip. After breakfast, Father saddled the donkey. It was a grey donkey with long, straight ears. When he nodded, he shook his ears, each ear in a different direction. Although the donkey didn't mind carrying shopping, he hated carrying children. As soon as Father sat a child on his back, he became restless. Father fed him carob beans, the donkey relaxed, and the children laughed. I thought the hills had never heard such excited children laughing so loudly before.

We moved slowly, Father led the donkey, and we followed, Ramón and Marcel-lí enjoyed the ride. The donkey stopped to pee and, further down the children needed to pee and later, the donkey stopped to poo. Step by step, we were leaving behind our house and its surrounding hills. Now and then a new ridge would appear in front of our eyes. Little by little, the town unfolded in front of us. Everything was new, and as we advanced, the crags got higher, and the grass edges were spotted with maiden pinks.

I left the group of walkers and ran off the path to pick a bunch. Their smell gave me a new life. Mother said they were a gift from heaven.

After some time, the children stopped laughing and began to complain that the journey was too long. After another stretch of walking, we saw a farmhouse at the foot of the hill. We heard the bells of cows grazing and then the cows. Having seen the house, the dogs began to bark, and the chickens ran helter-skelter.

Marcel-lí's Father and the landlady came out to greet us. I gave her the pinks before they faded. Father went back home alone, and we continued our walk among mountain crags. A stream appeared. It gurgled downhill, and as we passed a secluded pine forest, it disappeared under a footbridge only to surge out again with a more cheerful sound. We stopped to rest by a water spring with a footbridge.

The sun shone only on the tops of the highest ridges. Further down the path, the sun had sunk, and we lost the stream. The red-tiled roofs of houses with balconies spread down below. When I saw the towering Sant Francis's belfry, I felt small. We walked down some very rough steps made of old wood. Marcel-li's father had to carry him and soon after Josep had to shoulder Ramón. I could hardly keep my eyes open. We ended up in a dark, narrow street that reeked of fried fish and stale piss. Marcel-lí's older brother had grown into a good-looking teenager. He was the same age as Josep, his eyes big and grey, and his dark hair was cut short. A few black hairs grew on his face and, like Josep, his face was a little spotty. He hugged Marcel-lí' and kissed us all one by one.

In the morning, I awoke to the sound of church bells. The boys washed and got dressed. We met Marcel-lí's older brother, who was the same age as Josep and their aunt Pepeta. After kissing us all, she opened a drawer, got out a tablecloth and spread it on the table. I fell in love with the little flowers embroidered around the edges. Those flowers must have been the work of Marcel-lí's mother. It was like a message from her grave. If I ever had a baby girl, she would learn embroidery.

Since the day she came to our house to bring Marcel-lí, Pepeta had aged, her skin was pale, her eyes a little puffy. She wore a white blouse and a blue skirt. In the morning Mass men sat on the right, women on the left, the women dressed in soft tones and some girls wore white mantillas and white patent leather shoes. I thought they must be the shoes from their first communion.

After Mass, we met Marcel-lí's uncle Robert. He was taller than his Father, and two deep lines crossed his forehead. A few broken teeth at the front spoiled his smile, his eyelashes were invisible, leaving his brown eyes bare. His big, brown coat and shapeless trousers looked ready to fall from his thin body. But his white, Sunday shirt was clean and well-ironed. I didn't like the sound of his voice, and his handshake made me shudder. I felt a kind of deadness in his tobacco-stained and callous hands. He said he had to help to say Mass in Saint Francis church and left waving goodbye.

As we strolled down the high street, a strange whiff of perfume awoke new fantasies. I had never seen such elegant clothes. I looked at a bookshop, and I thought about the beautiful stories locked inside those colourful covers. I longed to see the pretty drawings of the children's books. In Saint Johns' square young people gathered in small groups in lively conversation and laughing. I wanted to know what made them laugh so loudly.

In the evening, Josep and Marcel-lí's older brother joined the crowd. We watched the festival from a balcony over the square. A small, fat man with a round, red hat began to beat a big drum; my heart began to pound, and my hands sweated. The boys stopped bickering and watched sitting on the balcony's floor, their hands holding tight on the railings. Marcel-lí smiled, and I watched in fascination as two dragons ran around spitting fire. Revellers ran in front of the dragon screaming and waving straw hats. The square was throbbing to the sound of music. Marcel-lí laughed, Ramón asked if the dragons would come up the stairs. Ernest followed the dragons as they roamed around the square spouting fire. When the dragons ran out of firecrackers, they were taken crestfallen back into the town hall. Instantly, four colourful dwarves sporting red and green, old-fashioned clothes walked into the middle of the square. They danced in intricate steps forming a ring, playing the castanets.

"Ho, ho! Big heads with square hats, " Marcel-lí laughed

"Look, look at the jumping steps," Ramón said, kicking his legs.

"The music is great!" Earnest added.

I felt out of this world. After the jolly dwarves, came the big, fat giants. They stepped forwards and backward wobbling, twirling till their velvety skirts swirled doing the real dance. I thought that being a dwarf was more fun than being a pompous giant. The lights went off and devils covered in the green leaves of clematis invaded the darkness. They had a bunch of firecrackers in their twisted horns—a good job I couldn't see their faces. Otherwise, I would have screamed in terror. Overwhelming drumming beats echoed around the square. Oh God, how I fretted, I was afraid that the balcony's floor would collapse and we'd all go down to the beat of a drum. The boys watched mesmerized with their small hands holding tight on the railings. The dark square was full of dancing devils with horns sparkling fire. The wild drumming got into my head, the devils' frantic dance was tiring, and the racket of exploding firecrackers left me numb. But there was more to come, the dragons, the eagle, giants, dwarves came back blending with people and forming a drunken whorl of maddening colours.

It took a long time before the revellers dispersed. Some disappeared into the side streets, others, sat on the church steps, holding their heads with both hands. The square was strewn with squashed ivy leaves and a stench of drink and gunpowder. That night I experienced the sleep of drunken people: loud music, a pool of bright colours, ugly faces and bad smells went around dancing inside my poor head. On the way back, it was all uphill, and we had to stop and rest. Having reached the farmhouse, we met Father with the donkey. Josep and Father began to discuss the harrowing war in Morocco. The war was costing thousands of young lives—wars, conflicts and more wars.

Chapter 7

Back home, up in the hills, the air was crispier than ever. While washing the boys' best clothes, images of life in the town appeared in my mind like visitors from another world. I imagined people dressed in their Sunday best, smelling of perfume, strolling up and down the high street. Then a festival dwarf came tottering among the crowd and stopped to look at the rich cakes in the shop window. I hoped that he had enough money. The most persistent image was the bookshop. I wondered what stories remained locked up inside those piles of books. I imagined the stories were like prisoners waiting for someone with the right key to open the book, and the characters inside would come to life. Small fairies would fly around, and elves would dance on the floor. And at a steamy corner, a half-hidden witch she was trying hard to cook another magic spell. Josep was passing with a basket full of hay and caught me giggling. As usual, he laughed, he probably thought that I was laughing for no reason. But I was laughing among silly dwarfs, happy fairies and a busy witch.

By the middle of July, the sky was clear, and the sun shone continuously every single day. At noon, the house was unbearably hot, flies moved around with ease, mated shamelessly and that wherever they fancied. Mother sprayed carbolic over the toiled and scullery, but the infuriating flies won the battle.

Outside, bluebottles' picket on the helpless cows. Small birds kept in the shade and the dogs slept in a cool spot at the back of the house. At times, the cry of a solitary magpie flying on its way to the forest would break the repetitive, grating chirping of the cicada. Down the path, the thorn had lost its blossoms and, in the meadow, the flowers were wilting away. I could hear the busy tiddling of small insects that seemed to have taken over the meadow. Bees and butterflies fed on the wispy flowers of purple thistles while lazy lizards choose to bask in the sun and gulped whatever insect that happened to be passing by. Life fed on life. It was a ruthless struggle for survival.

The men worked from sunrise to sunset reaping corn. I brought a lunch of dry sausage, bread and a porró full of wine in a wicker basket. They sat in the shade of an old, apple tree. The men eat, drunk discussed the fate of the country.

"As it happened our country was in turmoil," Father said. "The war with Morocco is killing our men."

The landlord gulped some more wine and asked.

"What can we do about it?"

"Not much, we're tied to Spain, and we have to do what they order, but now a new party called Estat Catalá has been founded that aims to claim independence, but Madrid doesn't like it."

"We shouldn't be expected to die to defend the king's mines and an empire that isn't ours." The landlord added.

I thought that the word empire meant something distant, dangerous and bizarre. Having finished the meal Father and the landlord lay on the grass. I picked up the empty basket and began to walk back. There was something strange in the middle of the path. The thing was green and coiled up. A repulsive feeling took over my body: it was a snake with a field mouse in its mouth. I picked up a big stone and threw it at the snake. The snake slithered into the bushes, and the poor mouse remained in shock. And I ran home with the feeling that the angry snake was chasing me.

Mother worried that with the boys growing up by next autumn, we wouldn't have enough milk. Father ordered two more cows from the dealer, and a few days later, two healthy cows arrived. One of the cows was already pregnant, and Josep took the cows to graze in a shady field that was still green below the oak. The kitchen smelled of sour milk, Mother was busy baking I moved about as in a state of sleepwalking. The intense heat, the constant squabbling of the boys and the fight against the flies left me in a state of sleepwalking.

By the end of August, the men had finished the arduous job of harvesting and threshing and then shifting the corn. When the corn was safe inside the landlord's house, we had the village feast. We waltzed till dark to the sound of an accordion. Some young people dared to dance the tango. After the Festa, the school holidays were over. Father would lose the boys' help and the boys their much-loved freedom.

"Everything comes to an end," Mother would say, "except poverty."

The boys returned to school, and Ramón began to spend time with our aunt Maria and her husband, Roc. He loved books and had lots in their house. The couple were childless, and they were happy to have him stay. I was busy changing the boys, beds, and I heard the cow's bells ringing. Josep was taking them out to graze. As I was about to finish picking up the dirty laundry, I heard trees breaking, the hill trembled, the dogs barked, birds flew away, and I wondered what could have happened. I went out to see what made such a terrifying sound of small trees breaking. I ran out to see what was happening: the big cow had fallen down the cliff. Josep was trying to move the little cow away from the washing and the big one strayed. The cow screamed in agony. The men rushed out; the cow struggled to stand up, but she just fell a little further down the cliff.

"She broke her back," the landlord said. He rushed into his house and came out with his hunting gun, and he shot the cow in the head to stop her suffering. I closed my eyes and Mother wiped her tears with her apron. Father held his head with his hands.

"Country life is full of such disasters." The landlord said.

Not long after, some black spots appeared in the sky, and the spots grew bigger and bigger until we saw vultures. I could hear their mighty wings flapping as the ugly birds descended swirling down one by one to feed on the unfortunate cow. First, they pecked greedily at the eyes and in the anus, forcing their way into her body.

Chapter 8

The snow fell again. The boys were out clearing the footpath, the dogs lay in the hay, and the sparrows hid under thick bushes. The mid-January sun was hot, and behind the snow-white peaks, the blue sky was radiant. After lunch, Father returned to the cowshed, and I went out to feed the leftovers to the dogs. Then the dogs came out of the barn and ran towards the path barking or my God! Robert was approaching. He trudged on the fresh snow with the help of a stick. He stopped to catch his breath. I rushed to tell Mother.

"Get some food for him," she said, drying her hands. Robert came into the house, sat in a chair and wiped his face. Father came in with the boys. Ramón and Marcel-lí we're expecting sweets. Robert's hands were holding tight the stick his, and his body shifted in the chair. Then, he looked at Marcel-lí and said.

"Dear boy, today...today I bring sad news," he said and took another deep breath.

"Your father has died."

"Do you mean... Manel is dead?" Father asked Robert nodded. It took some time before Father raised his right hand and slowly crossed himself, and we followed his example.

“It... it happened suddenly. It was the heart,” Robert said. Marcel-lí hid his face in Mother's apron, and she held him tight.

“Will say a mass for him," Father said, “It's God's will.”

Robert ignored the food on the table and soon left. It was going to take a long time to reach the main road. We went out to wave goodbye, but Marcel-lí stayed with Mother. A single rook settled on the barn.

The following Sunday, a special Mass was said in memory of Marcel-lí’s Father.

Sadly, tears made Marcel-lí’s blue eyes more beautiful. As the priest said the Latin prayers my body was numb, Marcel-lí sadness was seeping into my bones and remained staring at the bare walls: It was time to grieve, time to pray and ponder why life could abandon us in such a cruel manner.

As the spring rain was washing away the last snow over the mountains, the young cow went into labour. The cow screamed in pain all morning, refused water in the afternoon, and Mother sat with her all night. Early the next morning only the rain was heard. That day Father and the boys dug a hole for her and her unborn calf. In the evening, everyone was exhausted. After supper, we sat around the fire. Father rubbed his eyes and said.

"Jesus Christ, we don't deserve this!"

I rushed to stir the dying embers and stoke the fire.

"In this place, there’s only poor soil, dangerous precipices and bad luck," Father added.

Although Father always said that cities were a nest of sin, he began to search for a farmhouse near the town of Berga. I had forgotten how badly the streets smelled and welcomed the move as an opportunity to learn dressmaking. It didn't take long to find one. We loaded a cart with our belongings and moved out of that beautiful place where we had such bad luck.

Chapter 9

Our new home was a farmhouse called El Mass de Auget's. I could never have imagined that I was going to live in such a beautiful house. The big house had a row of large balconies on each floor with views beyond the Berga. But inside, every room needed repairs: walls cracked, old doors creaked, shutters dangled. The landlord said he'd do some repairs, but he must have forgotten all about the repairs. The threshing floor was right in front of the house. It had a row of thick bushes at the edge. Good! I thought, our cows would never fall down the rugged slope below.

At the back of the house, there was a steep mountain. Our Lady of Queralt's church was sitting on the top. A jagged line of steps zigzagged up the rocky mountain's side. It was a tough climb and three pretty, little shrines had been built on the way for people to rest, and pray.

In front of the house, the land sunk into a succession of terraced fields. They stretched down as far as the village. From the balcony, I could see part of the city in a background of low ridges and high, mountain peaks. A double line of plane trees ed the road that went from the town to St. Bartomeu's church and then, it disappeared into a bend. I wanted to see where it ended.

On a bright morning, I could spot things that I hadn't seen the day before: a white house on a green hill, a distant, craggy ridge fading into the blue distance. Yet, nothing was stranger than one of the trees outside. The tree was thin and tall. Its branches bent with clusters of silvery leaves and odd, seed pods that smelled of candy. Father said it was a Eucalyptus tree. The strange tree seemed frail; it heaved and creaked at the faintest gust of wind. It didn't feel safe. I thought that nothing could ever destroy the sturdy oak in front of our old house.

The boys were delighted in the new school because there were enough boys to make a football team. Josep got a job in a hotel situated in the village's centre, and he was pleased to earn some money. He bought fashionable clothes, and at weekends he went to town to dance the tango. Mother and I made cheese, bought eggs from the neighbours and on Saturdays, we loaded the donkey and went to the market to sell it for a small profit. When a housewife bought, cheese or eggs, Mother would ask them if they wanted to buy fresh milk. Soon we had gathered quite a few customers.

Going to sell the milk was very scary. From our new home to town was all downhill. But once I had reached the city, every voice, laugh, or whisper was a threat. Our customers lived in the old quarters of the town near St Aulalia's Church. I had to walk in stepped alleyways that connected each street to the next. I never knew what was going to appear in front of me. It could be a pitiful dog or a person saying good evening.

High up on the wall, every street had a quaint little shrine with a religious image. Carme street had a beautiful sculpture of our Lady of Carme. But in Pietat street the image was so sad that I had to look away. On my way back I could see the ruins of the castle and bats flew unexpectedly, over my head. We hadn't been in that house for long before we faced our first, sad episode that was going to remain in our hearts forever.

Chapter 10

The year 1925

It was Sunday Mass, and Robert hadn't shown up. It was very odd, I thought. The man was so creepy that I was terrified of him even in his absence. I glanced at the men's side: Father knelt holding his new cap in his hands. Josep was smiling at a girl, and it seemed that Ernest was pretending to pray. Marcel-lí was amusing himself by playing a game with his fingers. At the end of mass, two young girls stood at each side of the entrance hall, holding a tray of flowers. As the parishioners elbowed their way out, they would drop a coin on the tray, and the girl would give them a flower. The women took off their veils and folded them neatly. The men wore their flowers in their lapels, and the women would hold theirs over their folded veils. I was given a beautiful, red geranium but its bitter smell made me shiver.

Outside the church, some men headed straight into the coffee bar. Others, like Father, gathered around in idle conversation. Josep and his friends stood by the haystack laughing loudly. As the men began to talk about the independence of Catalonia, their voices became loud.

"Wars only benefit the king," the butcher said, "If we were independent, our men wouldn't be sent to the desert and be slaughtered like animals."

Desert? The only desert I knew was a pudding. I moved near the women who were discussing homemade remedies such as infusions of rude to get rid of children's threadworms. Young boys hid behind the cemetery gate, playing hide and seek. The crowd dispersed and walked back to their scattered farmhouses in a relaxed manner. We also walked up the hill to our house. The terraced fields were fringed with long grass; the tweeting sparrows flew from over the fields, and grasshoppers hopped away from the path.

For Sunday lunch we enjoyed a casserole of rice with rabbit. Josep went dancing the tango. The boys took the cows to graze up the hill. In the evening, Mother milked them, and then. When I got back from the town, the family was already saying the rosary. I was about to eat supper when Bang, bang, bang! Someone was knocking on the door.

"Something must have happened," Mother said.

"I'll go and see who is it," Father hung the rosary on the back of the chair and rushed downstairs. We heard Robert's loud voice.

"I've come to take Marcel-lí," he said.

"But it's late," Father said.

"I know," Robert added.

Marcel-lí tried to hide behind Mother, and Ernest began to cry. Heavy footsteps came up the stairs. I couldn't believe then, that Marcel-li was going to be torn away from us in such a cruel way. Robert and Father came into the dining room.

"It's time to take action," Robert said as he tried to grab Marcel-lí from the neck of his shirt.

"But it is ten o'clock," Mother said.

"Never mind the time. We're going," Robert said.

"Oh Lord, don't let it happen," I prayed. I wanted Father to kick Robert out of the house, but he said.

"Education is a good thing."

"He's only seven," Mother said.

"The earlier he gets onto the right path, the better," Robert said dragging Marcel-lí towards the door.

"What do you mean?" Father asked.

"Discipline, he needs discipline," Robert said.

"For God's sake, give him some time," Mother yelled.

"I'll run away," Marcel-lí shouted.

At that moment, I hated Father because he didn't stop Robert.

"If his father were alive," Mother sobbed, "he would have respected my opinion."

"Tears won't stop me from doing God's will," Robert said.

"Is it?" Josep asked, moving his head left and right.

To my dismay, Robert dragged Marcel-li downstairs, and we all followed them outside. The black-headed cow stood and watched. I was numb with rage, all the love and care we dedicated to him, and now we were powerless.

I wanted to follow them and be with Marcel-lí wherever he was going. Outside, a bat flew over my head; the air carried the smell of cows' dung. My strength was failing. Robert freed his hand from Marcel-lí's shirt and dragged him by the hand. We watched them going downhill, and soon we only saw two figures disappearing into the darkness. Mother sobbed, and I was heartbroken, that lovely baby we worked so hard to keep alive was being torn away so cruelly, out of our life.

Chapter 11

Solsona

We hurried downhill crying. When I tried to turn back, Uncle Robert tightened his grip on my arm.

“I know it’s tough, “he said, “but I have to do my duty to my dead brother.”

I cried louder.

“You must understand that if your Father ‘rest in peace,’ were here he would have taken you to Solsona himself.”

“I don’t believe that,” I mumbled.

“We couldn’t leave you to grow up without proper education. Tomorrow, our miners will have no supervision.”

Having reached the church and the cemetery, we turned right. An iron cross marked the road.

“We must keep to the side because the road is full of loose stones.”

A new moon peeped over the hill, and we could only see the road in front of us. I began to hear the sound of the waterfall and cried more. After crossing the bridge, Uncle Robert relaxed his grip, and I saw a flat field. It was so dark I couldn't see anything else. Then we walked by a forest of small evergreen oaks. The dwarf trees resembled real people and something spooky stirred from their shadows, and it fluttered over my head, as a little owl. It flew rising and swooping, going from tree to tree. I was grateful to the owl because the owl was sorry for me, he was following us. I had a friend.

When we reached another cemetery with cypress trees, I saw a tall belfry and a church. The owl settled on the church tower, I was afraid of losing him, but soon I heard him flying over us again. I could see cypresses and a bell tower. The owl was trying to show me the way back home.

We passed under three hills with round tops, and then we approached another stream, but his one had no bridge.

"Be careful here," Uncle said, as he began to pick his way stepping on each stone. I tried to follow his footsteps, but it was difficult because my legs were short. The water rushed between the boulders and fell, noisily, into a black hole hitting fallen tree branches and rocks on its way. I was afraid of being sucked into the gully, a few steps further on and my foot got stuck in a clump of rushes.

"Shit!"

"Mind your language boy," Uncle growled.

"I can't see properly," I replied, believing that I found solid ground, but I tripped on a crest of dry mud sticking from a rut. There were small water puddles shaped like cattle's hooves, reflecting the new moon.

"Don't stop, boy we have a long way to go."

A rocky outcrop followed. I wanted to run away to the mountains. My eyes began to close, and I tripped on every stone and every sod of earth that came our way.

"Keep walking, boy; we're nearly there ." Uncle Robert grunted.

"One day, you'll be grateful for today's hardship."

I threw myself onto the ground and cried.

"It's hard," Uncle said, "But it's worth it," I coughed.

Keep in mind that one day you'll come out of Solsona, a well-educated priest. You'll be a leader of men. There's nothing more worthy in this world than to take sinful men out of a life of sin and show them the path to God and eternity."

"I want to go back home," I sobbed.

"Your destiny is with your father's family now."

"I don't want a destiny."

He laughed.

Solsona is a town with a religious history; there's a lot to learn."

"I liked my school."

"We'll say the rosary and the Virgin Mary will to protect us during the journey."

"Ugh!"

"Haven't they taught you to respect in that house?"

"I'm sleepy!"

"Prayer will keep us awake."

"It's not working."

Uncle Robert got out a rosary from his pocket and began reciting the long prayer. I fell asleep on the grass.

I woke up with a cough, feeling cold and with insects crawling up my bare legs. I saw a single star and a big mountain in front of me. I was in another country.

We walked by ploughed fields, and a red glow appeared over the mountain and shortly after a new sun emerged. We walked for another hour or so and then, I saw a ghostly wall with a gate as black as a dragon's mouth.

"What's this?" I asked.

"That's Solsona," Uncle Robert replied, "The best city in the whole province of Lleida."

Good Lord, I was going to live behind that wall.

"See the building over the fortress," Uncle added.

"Do you mean those churches piled up one on top of the other?" I asked.

Uncle Robert laughed.

"It's a place dedicated to God, and you're very privileged to be able to come to study here."

After crossing the bridge, we found ourselves in the middle of a square with a few young plane trees and a pile of planks on the ground. Then we followed a narrow street, the houses were so high that you could hardly see the sky, and they had balconies with iron railings and flower pots. We reached 'Carrer del Angel', and Uncle knocked on the door. A middle-aged woman opened the door.

"Good morning Teresa! Here's the boy."

"Welcome home," she said.

She bent down and looked at me.

"Welcome home Marcel-lí," she said, passing her hand over my hair.

"Hello," I mumbled.

"Oh, you have blue eyes like your father's," she said.

"You have no idea how my brother and I longed to see this day."

I had just spent a terrible night walking in the dark.

"We wanted so much to have you home with us. But you must be exhausted, poor little thing."

Aunt Teresa's black dress was so long that I could only see the tip of her black shoes. Her face was thin, and her eyes were not black, neither brown, just plain dull. Her grey hair was too flat; the skin under her eyes puffy and her perfume tickled my nose.

"We need a wash," Uncle Robert said.

We walked through a dining room with a long table, six chairs and a painting of the last supper on the wall. Outside, the sun was rising, and I was falling asleep. My life had gone topsy-turvy. Uncle and I sat at the table, and Aunt Teresa served breakfast. The omelette was good, and the bread with tomatoes tasted delicious. But the milk was watery. As I was going to bed, my foster brothers were running downhill to school, and without me. Uncle Damia arrived home.

"Marcel-lí is here," said Aunt Teresa.

"Welcome to our family Marcel-li," he said.

"Hello, Uncle," I replied.

"You're a big boy now, and you need to learn discipline."

I was terrified of discipline.

Chapter 12

In the evening we went to see the Cathedral. The street was so narrow that the sun never reached it. The Cathedral's big door opened with a loud squeak, inside it was dark and creepy. Behind the big altar, there was a red curtain, the pews were empty, but for an old woman whispering a prayer.

"This is the house of God," Uncle said, passing his right hand over a pew.

"Why is it so dark?" I asked.

"No need for light because people come here to seek peace with God."

I didn't like the way he spoke. We followed to a chapel on the side.

"This chapel is dedicated to our lady of the Cloister," Uncle said in front of a dark image surrounded by angels.

"I like the angel's golden wings," I replied.

"Yes, they're well painted," he said, and we crossed over to the other side

"This chapel is dedicated to Mare de Deu de la Mercer. It's a baroque masterpiece," Uncle added. She had a lot of decorations around and a saint on each side. The candles at her feet were red, but only one candle remained lit.

"In the morning, while I prepare the mass, you're going to lit the candles."

That night I went to bed with a headache.

A frightening knock startled me awake. It was still dark. I remembered that Uncle had told me the night before that we were going to start early. I stumbled out of bed, washed and dressed as quickly as I could. Uncle was waiting for me as we walked towards the Cathedral I had to run to catch up with his long steps. When we reached big door Uncle bent down, pushed in the key the door opened. The Cathedral was darker than the night before, and no one was inside; it smelled of rotting wood.

Uncle knelt in front of the altar, and I did the same. I followed him to the room behind the altar called sacristy, but I lost him. I found him again rummaging inside a cupboard full of clothes; he turned towards me and gave me a black cassock.

"Try this," he said, and I put it on obediently, over my usual clothes.

"Too big," I said.

"You'll soon grow into it."

"But I step on the hem," I replied.

"Haven't they taught you to say thanks?"

"Thank you, Uncle," I mumbled, swallowing my tears. Then Uncle gave me a white chasuble to wear over the cassock while helping in Mass.

"I'll teach you the differences between each Mass," Uncle said." There are the Communion Mass, the Whitsun Mass and the Pentecostal Mass. Every Mass requires a different colour vestment, but don't worry about remembering the right colour for the time being."

I didn't worry; I wasn't going to learn any of that. Uncle's early Mass ended, but to my horror, a canon was already waiting to say another mass. I was so hungry I could barely stand on my feet. As that Mass ended, another canon came in, and the masses didn't stop till eight o'clock.

Uncle Damia and I went home for breakfast. The bread was not was too soft, the milk tasteless. Uncle only drank a glass of milk and then went back to the Cathedral. Aunt Teresa tidied the breakfast table.

"We're going to the barber for a haircut," She said, taking off her apron. In the barbershop, I sat in a big chair.

"Keep your head down," the barber said. And I was turned into a sheep.

“Now we’re going to the tailors.” We walked along a dark and narrow street leading

to nowhere.

The tailor’s shop was small, and it had a desk with patterns, measuring tapes coiled round and the biggest scissors I had ever seen. The tailor had white hair and silver-rimmed glasses. He measured my shoulders, made a note and then my arm and elbow.

“A big boy for his age,” he said. The measuring tape went over my bare knee, I squirmed like a worm, and he laughed. Aunt Teresa frowned.

A few days later, my suit was ready for collection, the tailor had turned the cloth of a retired army general’s jacket inside out, and it looked new to me.

“It’s too big,” I protested.

"You'll soon grow into it," replied Aunt Teresa sullenly.

In the evening I had a surprise: Uncle gave me a little box with pencils and a fountain pen and a square-shaped bottle of ink. I tried out, but the ink ran out before I could finish a word. The following day Aunt took me to visit the school. In that uncomfortable coat, I felt like a ridiculous clown. The school was a big house with elegant windows on the top floor; a man dressed in a black tunic and a big, white-collar.

"Welcome to your new school Marcel-li," he said. He led us upstairs to an office with a large black and white picture on the wall.

"That's Saint John Baptist of la Salle. He was the founder of our order," he said.

Aunt Teresa smiled.

"He dedicated all his life to teaching poor children. He was a firm believer that children should be taught in their mother tongue."

I started school with the teacher, Brother Ignasi calligraphy in Castillian. Later in the playground, a boy asked, laughing.

"Where's your sword, my general?"

"You wait, and you'll see," I said, raising my fist.

"You're taking it too seriously boy," Lluis said, "We always make fun of each other's clothes or the way some boys speak. It helps to pass the time."

Although I took the mickey out of stupid boys myself, I was angry. When, finally, the class ended, we elbowed out of the old building like chickens running out of the coop. As soon as we were out I tapped Lluis on the shoulder, and I said, "Let's run," Lluis started to run as fast as he could, and I flowed him, and we run and laugh out the town. Up the hill, we stopped. Lluis got a catapult out of his pocket and started to shoot at the sparrows feeding on a field. The whole flock flew away at once and settled dwarf oak.

"Wow, boy! I want to try it."

I tried it, but the stone fell on my foot, I returned the catapult to him ashamed of my clumsiness.

"Last summer, I shot a snake dead. I also shot sparrows and then ate them for supper. I love them with rice."

"I must get home now. I live in farmhouse further up," Lluis said, pointing at the hills. Hills meant freedom and I missed my foster mother's house. The town's clock stroke, Lluis left. I had a strong urge to follow him out of that stinky town. At the edge of a field, I saw a dead toad. I picked it up, put it in my pocket and began to run back but followed a different street. A scared cat passed me by, and I felt trapped. An old lady walked up with a country loaf under her arms and no sign of Uncle's street. After wandering around for some time I ended up in front of the Cathedral, I looked around, I saw no one I dropped the toad at the entrance. I recognised Miquel Street.

At last! I found Uncle's house. I knocked on the door; Aunt Teresa appeared looking angry.

"How come you're so late?" she asked.

"Oh, I got lost," I replied.

"But the school is not that far, and you could have asked the way home," she said, putting her hands to her waist," everyone knows where we live."

"I wanted to see the town."

"No excuses, you've got to remember to come home straight from school otherwise. I'll tell your Uncle." We went upstairs to her seating area Aunt sat in a chair, picked up a pair of scissors and began to cut the pages of the newspaper into squares for the toilet. Then the bells began to toll for the dead. We crossed ourselves. I remembered the frog and turned my face stifling a giggle. Uncle returned late with a worried look.

"Old Rosa has died," Uncle said.

"Poor Rosa; may her soul rest in peace," Aunt sighed, "she came to this world to suffer."

"Yes, she did, she had been ill for as long as I can remember, but God will take her to heaven."

"It's God's will."

"It was a hard day in the Cathedral and, to end it all, there was a dead toad at the entrance," Uncle sighed.

"A toad?" asked Aunt Teresa.

"Yes, a toad," replied Uncle.

I began to worry.

"Perhaps it walked there in the night," I said.

"No, it had been dead for a couple of days. It was some sort of a joke," replied Uncle.

"I remember when some naughty boys left a dead snake by the fountain. Poor Marina had a real fright, "said Aunt Teresa.

"Wicked boys," replied Uncle.

Oh, dear, what I've done, I will have to confess to my Uncle about the dead toad. Since I didn't know how I'd get out of that, just forget it, I said to myself.

At dinner time we had potatoes and cabbage mashed together. The bacon's rind was crispy. It cracked between my teeth the way I liked. But the thought of Lluis eating sparrows with rice made me very envious, and even if he made me a catapult and I learned to shoot sparrows Aunt wouldn't want to cook them.

Chapter 13

It was a lucky day. Aunt Teresa ran out of sugar, and she told me to go out and buy some. I grabbed the opportunity to walk around the old city. I had learnt that tangle of narrow streets all leading to Saint John's Square. I just bumped into Martí, the boy who had laughed at my clothes. I wasn't going to waste the opportunity. I grabbed him like a fox catching a chicken, pushed him to the ground and instead of fighting back, the idiot screamed. I beat him hard on the head and the chest. A shopkeeper heard him and rushed to help him.

"Wicked devil," shouted the shopkeeper taking Marti by the hand and helping him back to his feet.

"He's a bloody coward," I shouted back. The shopkeeper took him into his shop. I continued walking and soon forgot about it. But in the evening, Uncle Damia gave me the first beating.

"It's a disgrace," he said, slapping my face. I shrugged my shoulders.

"We are not ordinary people, boy," he followed, "our behaviour must be a perfect example to the people of this town. Do you understand that?"

"Yes," I replied.

"Yes or no is not good enough here. You must say yes, Uncle or yes Sir, people have a title.

"Yes, Uncle, but he shouldn't have laughed."

"Remember Jesus on the cross; did he hit back?"

"No, Uncle."

"Did Jesus laugh at those who taunted him while he was suffering on the cross?"

"No Uncle, but"

"What?"

"I think he should have run away."

"If he had run away, we wouldn't have had our religion. We would be living in complete darkness. You must repent and pray for forgiveness."

Since we prayed all day, I wasn't going to pray anymore. Uncle locked himself in his study. Aunt Teresa was sad. As consolation for my beating, she gave me her hand and took me to her room. I saw a statue of a nun on top of a chest of drawers.

"She is St Teresa," Aunt said, "I owe my name and my faith, and I follow her guidance. Her faith was so strong that she could see God in the cooking pot."

I wondered what God was doing in the cooking pot, but I didn't say anything.

"She looks like a nun," I replied fearing that we were going to end up praying again.

"Yes, she was a nun the founder of the Carmelite order, and she wrote the book of prayers, she is holding it in her hand."
I nodded.

"The book is the perfect path to bliss."

"I don't know what bliss is?" I told.

"Oh, it's a state of being at one with God."

"I like climbing trees with my friends."

"There's no need to climb anything when you can rise above the ordinary with prayer."

I knew we were going to get into that.

"I pray every evening; the first stage is what she called mental prayer, then the Prayer of Quiet, and the Reunion with God."

Aunt Teresa remembered the potatoes boiling on the stove, and she hurried out of the room. I was confused by so many words. I missed the thrill of discovering a bird's nest, climbing a mountain and seeing the forest stretching in front of me.

Aunt Teresa went to do the washing in the communal washing tub. I took the opportunity to search for God inside the cooking pots. I opened several pots, big and small, and I saw nothing but emptiness. Disappointed, I went into Uncle's bedroom. I wasn't allowed inside Uncle's bedroom; I grabbed the opportunity to have a good look at it. He had a small bed, a chest of drawers with a big book on it, a big painting of St Dominic of Guzman on the wall and to my disappointment nothing else. The room smelled of mothballs, and I left.

Despite all the masses and prayers, a suffocating feeling of emptiness grew inside me. Nothing in that place could fill up. I thought that Uncle got his strength and happy mood from the holy wine he drank during Mass. So I had the idea of taking a little sip of the wine, and I too would feel happy. It worked, I swallowed some wine, and It cheered me up instantly; Holy wine was the best wine I had ever tasted. It was so good that on Tuesday I took a bigger sip and the following day, a little more.

On Saturday day, one of the priests who came to say Mass saw me and told Uncle. The priests preach forgiveness, but what they dish out is only punishment. I got another beating.

"I've been working all day, and I had to suffer that humiliation," he shouted. And he slapped my bottom. I didn't cry.

"Today, I let it pass," Uncle added, "another day you'll go to bed without supper."

The daily Masses were so dull that as we walked away from the altar, I danced a few steps in the hope that no one would see me. I was dancing in my long cassock. But some old woman who allowed her mind to wander off the holy prayer told my Uncle. He beat me again, but he let the woman go free.

Slowly and slowly, I was dying, dying right under the eyes of the Virgin on the main altar, and the rest of the saints on the side chapels. There was no point in praying to them because I had the feeling that they were all on Uncle's side. I had to do something very quickly. I began to plan my first escape. I would steal some food and climb out of my room in the night, and the next morning I'd be in my foster mother's house. I chose a full moon night because I will be able to see the mountains and church steeples to guide me. The trip was going to be very exciting, and I might see my friend the owl.

Chapter 14

I had to learn that I wasn't a girl like the others; in the city, I was an ignorant country girl. I remember the evening when some boys jumped at me saying. "Oh, look! What a pretty peasant."

I felt insulted. The next morning, I told Mother.

"Well, we're country people," Mother said while washing the milk pots, "remember Bernadette she was illiterate and when someone called her ignorant she replied. 'I can still love God more than anyone else.'"

I wished I were a Bernadette with the right reply for every situation in life.

One evening, I had a surprise, when I went to sell the milk a young man came to open the door.

"Come in please," he said, "my mother is not in today." He disappeared into the kitchen and returned with the milk pan. He looked at me and said.

"What's your name?"

"Rosana," I said.

"Beautiful!"

"Thanks."

"Rosana your face's gone red?"

I didn't know what happened to me but, as I held the measuring jug, my hands shook and spilt milk on the floor.

Oh God! How clumsy I felt! But he just got a cloth from the kitchen and wiped the floor laughing. I had never seen the men cleaning anything, and I couldn't stop giggling. I rushed out of the door. On the stairs, the light had gone, and I was still giggling. I went down, feeling my way with my hand on the wall, step by step into the darkness. At the last step, I tripped on the flat floor. The empty pot hit the wall, and it clung like the bell of mountain cows. I walked as fast as I could along the stepped, narrow streets and up the hill. Over the town's roofs, a waning moon was sailing between two clouds.

The next morning as I was fanning the coals to make the pot boil, I told Mother about the man I met the night before.

"Last night I met a young man."

"Well, I'm not surprised; there are lots of young men out there." She said peeling a potato.

"Yes, but that man was different, he wore a white shirt."

"I must warn you about city men. They're smartly dressed and dance the tango, but they have no intentions of marrying country girls."

"Oh, but why not?"

"Well...we only know how to look after cows," Mother said, raising her head.

"Not very useful in a town," I said, breaking a long branch into smaller twigs.

"And being illiterate, what could we do?" Mother moved her head sideways.

"But you said that although we were illiterate, we could still love God.

"Yes, and bring up children."

"Do you think I'll get married?"

"I hope so you must have your kitchen."

"It's that all then?"

"Not all but it's an awful situation to have to share a kitchen. Imagine Josep marrying three women here, his wife would want to please Josep, and I have to please Father. Do you understand?"

"Yes, I do, but Josep wouldn't marry yet," I said.

"No. We've no money," Mother began to knead a bit of fat with flour and make a dumpling.

"Well then, we can be the kitchen queens a little longer."

Mother laughed.

In the night I thought of the man with a white, open shirt, the sleeves up to the elbow, and how I liked the way he moved around the house, his hair was dark and straight and was falling carelessly over his broad forehead.

Chapter 15

That Sunday Mass, the priest wore purple, with a stole embroidered in gold. I loved the colours. Mass was in memory of the dead soldiers in the war with Morocco. Ramón came that day and sat in the men's row next to Father. He wore a new grey suit and blue necktie; his hair was short. His tie was long and hung awkwardly out of his jacket. But his child's voice followed the Latin Mass word for word with concentration.

I could never learn the Latin Mass by heart and, hearing him, I felt clumsy. I just repeated what other people said; my voice was nothing but an echo. Josep was looking at the girls, and Ernest kept doing and undoing the buttons on his sleeve. It was a relief when the priest turned his face to the congregation and gave the final blessing. I heard the words 'Go with peace.' Everyone stood, sighed and crossed. The young people jostled between the rows of pews heading for the door in a desperate rush to get out. I wished to get out and join my new friends, but courage failed me. Older people walked out with slow steps as if regretting having to leave behind the comfort of their seats.

Outside, there was the usual after Mass gathering. Viviana was folding her veil while Lola was playing with her marjoram twig. Carmen waved to me. Children ran around a group of men discussing the war. Father stood listening. Lluis, the butcher, was dressed in a navy-blue suit.

"This war is costing us far too much," he said, stamping his foot.

"Yes, but the king wants his mines," Father added.

"If we were masters of our destiny, this tragedy wouldn't have happened," Lluis said.

"Independence is the solution," Josep said.

Father bit his lip. Ernest was talking to a friend in front of the inn. Churchgoers began to disperse. Some families followed the stone wall that led to the village. Others walked along a path between the freshly ploughed fields. We walked up the hill, at a leisurely pace, enjoying the fresh air and the warm midday sun. On the edges of the terraces, the grass was dry, but clusters of tiny, white yarrow blossoms stood out fresh and lovely. The purple thistle rustled; my new dress whispered in the wind. As we approached the house, I began to think of the sweet cinnamon taste of the custard we were going to have for dessert.

"I can't see the puppy," said Mother.

"That's strange," replied Father.

"Perhaps he's run away," said Josep.

"No, he was well tethered," said Ernest.

"Oh, look! Someone has left a coat under the eucalyptus," said Father.

"We only have one coat," I replied. Then I saw the puppy jumping around.

"Good Lord!" Mother screamed.

"What's happening?" Father asked.

"Look, who's here!" replied Josep.

Marcel-lí stood up from the bed of dead leaves under the eucalyptus.

"Marcel-lí," Ernest shouted.

We stopped. Marcel-lí flung himself into Mother's arms.

Father's face tensed.

"You ran away," he said.

"Marcel-lí nodded.

"Let's go inside," said Father.

"And how did you get here?" asked Ramón.

"On foot," Marcel-lí sobbed.

"Dear, God," Mother said.

Father opened the door. Inside the house, the fire had died out. I rushed to change my clothes. Mother brought milk for Marcel-lí. I made a tower of dry twigs lit a piece of pine kindle and fanned it till I got it flaring.

"Here you are boys," I said. Marcel-lí sat by it to warm himself up.

"What a way of shivering," Mother said.

"Rossana, tonight you must go to tell his Uncle that Marcel-lí's here," said Father.

"Oh, don't tell them," said Marcel-lí, "they'll come and beat me up."

"No one's going to beat you up," said Father.

"Let's get lunch," said Mother.

We had chopped and fried the rabbit the day before, so Mother just added rice, a bay leaf and water to the casserole. She began to fan the stove, and I laid the table while listening to Father's and Marcel-lí's conversation.

"So, tell us about the trip to Solsona," Father said.

"It was long, and I was tired, but I liked the sounds of the night. After a few walking hours, we stopped to sleep on the grass. When we woke up covered with insects."

"Yak" Ramón squirmed.

"We shook off the ants, and we continued until dawn when a wall appeared in front of us. A big roof poked out on the other side, and Uncle said that was the Cathedral."

"I would love to see it," Ernest said.

"It's an awful place."

"It's the cathedral of the dioceses," Father said.

"It smells mildew and dead bodies," Marcel-lí added.

"The cow's shed smells of shit, "Father said.

"But shit is life, the Cathedral is cold and very dark, and no matter how many candles I light, it remains dark. Dark, dark, dark I was dying right in front of the eyes of our Lady Mother of God."

I was chopping the salad onions and cried. Mother put the casserole at the centre of the table, and I brought out a plate with lettuce, onion and the last fresh tomatoes of the year.

"The celebration of Mass is to help us live in harmony with God and each other," Father said, taking a spoonful of rice from the steaming casserole.

"I never understood religion," Josep said.

Father frowned.

"I won't mind living with intelligent people," Ramón said.

"Oh, they all say the same thing," Marcel-lí said.

"Not at the same time, I hope." Ernest laughed.

"I suspect what life there is like here, people on top know it all and the rest of us nothing. We work all day for them to eat they call us ignorant peasants," Josep said.

"You're sowing rebellious and anarchic influences," Father said.

"It's the truth," replied Josep.

"You're not going to join one of those unions where people think that they can do away with the King, church and legal systems and replace it with a load of noisy tango dancers like you," Father said.

"We need change, but the landowners fear it, "said Josep.

Marcel-lí coughed. Mother looked worried.

I got up from the table to collect the dinner plates. Marcel-lí was still picking at the rabbit bones. He liked to chew the gristle in the ribs. Mother brought in the custard, and I laid out the pretty small blue plates and ladyfinger biscuits. Delicious.

Chapter 16

On Friday morning Marcel-lí played with the puppy. But in the evening, just before I was leaving for the milk round, someone rushed into the house.

"Where is he?" Robert shouted. Father rushed to confront him.

"The boy's ill," Father replied.

"Come out at once!" He bellowed, "Or I'm going to kill you."

"Not in front of me," Father said.

"You hide him."

"We're only looking after him."

"This complacency jeopardised his education," Uncle hit the table with his first.

"I said the boy's ill."

"I demand to see him immediately."

Mother and I hid in Marcel-lí's room.

"Get ready boy we're going to my house and tomorrow early in the morning we'll walk back to Solsona."

"I want to stay here," Marcel-lí replied.

"You already had a break. Now it's time to get to work," Robert said. Father came up from the stables.

"Marcel-lí, do as you're told," Father said.

"I don't want to go!" Marcel-lí kicked the door, "I hate that place."

"You have to and don't you dare to do another runner because your foster parents won't have you in this house."

"I never said that," Mother added, "Marcel-lí is my child, he can come back home any time he likes."

"You're spoiling his education," Uncle Robert shouted.

"First, we must become human beings and then educated persons."

Mother sounded very angry.

"Filomena don't you intervene," Father said.

"I brought him up, and now I can't even say what I think," Mother said.

"His needs have changed. He no longer needs milk. Now, he needs education." Uncle Robert replied.

"I hate that place, and I hate you. I'll hate you for the rest of my life." Marcel-lí screamed. I gave him a hanky and cried with him.

"You've got to respect people's nature." Mother said.

"We have to do God's will and forget nature," Robert added.

"I thought nature was created by God, for our wellbeing," Mother said.

"Don't forget that between God and nature, the devil is trying to frustrate God's will," Robert said.

"If you push it down his throat, he would be sick," Mother added.

"Enough talk!" Father said, "Change your clothes and go with your Uncle."

I remembered the silence, and then, the anger in Marcel-lí's face as he came out of the room. I was so afraid. I thought his uncle would beat him. But his Uncle grubbed him by the hand and marched him out of the house. We followed them out crying.

"Goodbye, Marcel-lí," Mother sobbed.

"Make the best of a good education boy and good luck," Father said.

"This would have an unhappy end."

"Stop making predictions."

Father walked to a nearby field and made a bonfire with dry potato stacks. A cloud of smoke soon blurred the view, and the snails and insects sheltering in the stacks exploded in the fire. Years went by, and Marcel-lí would turn up at our house, and his uncle would come a few days later. Robert threatened to get the civil guard, Marcel-lí, and said he would run away, Mother argued with Robert and Father with Mother. Father said that the law was on their side, and we had no right to intervene. Rage, rage, the rage of the powerless that ends with tears.

But my tears didn't wash away my sadness. On the contrary, the sadness left my body numb and exhausted. I sat outside watching Marcel-lí disappearing downhill and feeling the wind blowing in my face and dry my tears.

Chapter 17

I was going for a sewing session that day, so I didn't have to do any washing. Right after lunch, I changed my dress and strode downhill singing. “María De Les Trenas." The song tells the story of a girl's golden plaits, but when she marries and becomes a mother, she cuts them. The dry, wind blew my skirt, and on the path, the grass had dried, and tall spikes of dog leaves creaked with rusty seeds. A flock of twittering sparrows flitted past and descended on a terraced field in front of me. By the way, I still had a few sweets left over from my fourteenth birthday in my pocket and a few coins. Mother gave me to buy some minced to make meatballs.

Having reached the house, I found the front door open, but I still knocked. Viviana came down with slow steps and a soft smile.

"Hi, you must be Rosana," she said.

"Yes, that's me."

"Well, come up and meet the other girls."

There was the sweet smell of carob pods coming from a cupboard under the stairs. Viviana began to climb the first steps, and I noticed a few silvery lines shining in her black hair. She wore a straight-blue dress with a white, pointed collar made of delicate lace. On the first floor, there was a mirror on the wall that reflected part of Viviana's face. Her skin was pale, her eyes, coal-black with a spark of light, but as she looked ahead, I saw a hint of sadness in her face. Two girls of about my age sat by the window one girl smiled, and the other stopped her sewing and said hello.

"Sit down," Viviana said, pointing at the chair by the window. She picked a heavy coat from the sewing table and left it on my lap.

"Whipstitch this hem," she said.

I threaded the needle with the white cotton, and I began the long stitch. The plush material was warm, and a strange feeling grew between my legs. Viviana set to work with the sewing machine. The repetitive run-run-run of the machine increased my excitement. The machine moved fast. Each stitch in the row came out straight. How wonderful, I thought. The room smelled of new material like a shop, and I sneezed.

"My sister is getting married," Carme said, smiling."

At home, our lives have gone upside down.

"Oh, that's nice. I love weddings. I hope to be invited," Lola said.

"Well if they don't invite you to their wedding, you'll be invited to mine," Carme said with her eyes on her sewing.

"You mean your wedding?" Lola beat her lips and said.

"Yes, I do mean my wedding."

"You're moving fast," Carme added, "you don't even have a boyfriend."

"Well, Pau waits for me."

"Does he wait for you? I wonder," Lola laughed.

"Huh, you're taking the piss," Carme said.

Viviana's feet worked the sewing machine non-stop and laughed.

"Getting married is not everything," she said.

"Well, that's what my mother says," Lola added threading her needle and making a knot at the end.

"So much excitement over nothing on her wedding night the experience was painful, her period started, and it ended in tears."

"Oh! God," Carme shouted,

I squirmed.

"Well, that's life the way God created it, mess and all," Viviana sighed. At the end of the session, Carme looked out from the window, saw Pau and rushed downstairs to say goodbye. As Lola and I walked downstairs, she said.

"Viviana's sister died of childbirth." A strange silence followed

We walked in silence till we reached a footpath and a small waterfall. Under the waterfall, a spring was flowing into a lively stream. The stream soon ended in a communal washing tub.

Lola pointed at two women scrubbing clothes and said.

"Here's we do the laundry and gossip."

She said hello to the women. Then we passed the restaurant where Josep worked. Outside, an awning flapped over small square tables with beautiful pink tablecloths. A monstrous dog rose from a dark corner and barked ferociously. I cringed, Lola giggled, and the dog went back to sleep.

On the left, there was a farmhouse with a water fountain and a drinking trough on the wall. On the right, there was a square with an inn with lots of windows and further up a hotel. The road began to slant. Lola said goodbye and disappeared behind a single row of brick houses. There was a stream of donkey piss trickling down the stony path and a donkey, tied to the wall with a bag of carob pods hanging from its neck. The butcher was struggling to skin a dead sheep, and there was a puddle of blood on the ground. The shop smelled of fresh blood. I bought the meat to put a sweet in my mouth and walked home. As I reached the house, I found a puppy playing on the steps. Mother told me that our neighbours had given it to us. Ernest decided to call the puppy "Brú." The puppy amused himself, scaring the chickens and poor Brú lost his freedom; because he got tethered to the eucalyptus tree.

The following Friday, Mother gave me some money, and I had my hair cut in a fashionable style. When I went to deliver the milk in Carrer de la Pietat, my customer Veronica opened the door and said.

"Oh, how pretty you look!"

Oriól came out of the kitchen and Veronica went to fetch the milk pan.

"Mother said you wanted to ask me something about Robert?" Oriól asked.

"Yes, well... at home, we are worried about Marcel-lí. His uncle took him to Solsona. Mother's afraid that he won't be happy there."

"I heard about that, but I don't know anything except the local gossip. If I see one of the workers, I'll l ask whether they've heard anything. There's no point in asking him directly. He's a strange man, a bit of a fanatic."

I didn't know what fanatic meant, but, I was sure it meant something bad. Veronica returned from the kitchen with the milk pan. I poured the milk into the pan, and put the lid back on. I felt ill at ease and disconcerted, said goodbye and left.

"Goodbye and take care on your way home," said Veronica.

"I'm going for a drink," Oriól said.

"Don't come back too late," Veronica said.

"I won't," he replied. He walked by my side for a moment and then disappeared.

When I told Mother that Oriól had called Marcel-lí's Uncle Robert a fanatic, she looked upset."

"So, you saw that man again?"

"Well, yes, he was at home with his mother," I said.

"Try not to be left alone with him."

"I don't understand, why not?"

"You're a woman now, you have to take care of yourself, and you mustn't be seen with men. It could ruin your prospects of making a good marriage."

Chapter 18

Just as I had forgotten all about Uncle Domenec, he turned up, unexpectedly to the house. He surprised us in the middle of cheese making. As usual, Brú barked, but this time we heard Father laughing loudly. Mother rushed to wash her hands, and I looked out from the balcony. I saw Uncle Domenec. He had returned from Rome., our Uncle was a priest in charge of a Shrine up in the mountains of La Nou. Father and uncle came upstairs, and after the usual greetings, Uncle looked at me.

"How beautiful you have grown," he said.

I looked away.

"And tell us, how was Rome?" Father asked.

"Oh, Rome, Rome is a unique city. There is art and history everywhere, incredible city," he said.

"Oh well... as you can see, here, all chicken shit scattered all over the place," Father said, Uncle smiled. He looked much older; the hair at the back of his bald head was now, almost snow white. His skin was pale, his round face soft, with few lines at the corner of his eyes and the sides of his mouth. But his sharp grey eyes hadn't lost any of their youthfulness. Uncle looked smart and respectable. His black cassock was impeccable, his black shoes well-polished and his fingernails clean. It was hard to believe that Uncle and Father had grown up in the mountains together. How I admired Uncle's manners, the way he moved his soft fingers and what surprised me most was his smile: instead of guffawing the way local men did, he smiled without opening his mouth. One could see clearly that Uncle Dominic was not an ordinary man: God had blessed him with the power to absolve sin.

Mother told me to go and get some food. When I returned with a plate of bread and dry sausage, I found that Father's mood had changed, he was no longer laughing, and Mother was staring at the floor.

"It's a poor parish, but it would be well cared for," Uncle said.

"I'm sure our sister would be happy to have him."

I sensed something bad was about to happen. Ernest came through the door with his school books under his arms.

"Here he is," Father said.

"Hello, Uncle Domenec." Ernest rushed to kiss his hand.

"Have some food." Mother said and gave Ernest a slice of bread and a piece of dry sausage.

"Uncle needs help to mind the cows," Father said.

"Just think about it." Mother added.

"You would be paid a small salary, enough to buy clothes and books," Uncle said.

"Yes, I would like to try it," Ernest replied, thinking about having books and money.

That was it: Uncle came to Ernest away from us. At that moment, I hated his compliments, his good manners, and his elegant fingers. Before he left, Uncle gave us a handful of booklets with pictures of Rome. Ernest and I looked at the photos of that far-away place. I found it very strange. Ernest explained the city seemed to have more ruined buildings and statues than people. In the next, the beautiful fountain of Trevi was continuously flowing in fancy spouts and wasting water. On the next page, Romans were laughing as Christians were beings fed to lions.

"I don't believe that such cruel people ever existed," I said.

"Oh, yes," Ernest added, "it's true. We had studied the history of Rome in our class not long ago. All that happened in Rome before Christ. "

The following weekend, Father took Ernest to Uncle Dominic's church up in the hills of La Nou. Mother became forgetful, and sometimes I found her wandering into the boys' rooms, took a look around and came out again, saying that the house was too big. Being Father's little woman was full of pain, without Ernest, who would explain the world to me?

Chapter 19

The Requiem Mass

In Solsona the cathedral had been specially cleaned that Saturday. The altar had fresh, white lilies and new candles.

The deceased had been very generous to the Cathedral, and we had to do our best: but I was tired. Father Silvestre and Father Anselm came to sing the Latin Chants. Father Anselm was young, tall and laughed for no reason. He moved with ease, and his laughter brought a spark of life into the ancient cathedral. Father Silvestre was old, and small and needed help to put on the religious vestments. The bells tolled for the last time, uncle walked to the altar and followed him. I could hear Father Silvestre's frail bones creak inside the stiff, black chasuble. But his mass of healthy white hair looked smashing. The priests hang the stoles around their necks. "Eternal rest grant them, O, Lord". Uncle said, and the funeral Mass began.

The cathedral was full of people dressed in black, sobs, cries and coughs mingled with uncle's Latin prayers. White hankies had never been more useful. My mind was with my friends out in the square playing football. Martí, another altar boy nudged me on the elbow. Oh dear, I almost forgot the incense. I fetched the incense, the priests sang, "Santos Sanctus Sanctus," and spread the smoke. I picked up the burner from uncle's hand with a sneeze and swung it a little longer when Dear God! a black fly was fluttering from lily to lily. I just didn't know what to do. I needed fresh air.

At last, Uncle said "Lux Eterna." The fly vanished, and the Mass ended. Inside the sacristy, I helped Father Silvestre and hung the vestments into the cupboard. Father Anselm turned around and said.

"So, it seems that country's going to the dogs."

Father Silvestre's left hand began to shake. He grabbed it with the right one and staffed it into his left pocket. Uncle pulled a chair from his writing desk and said.

"Sit down Father Silvestre."

"Where else could we go?" He said as he sat. "The king is mad about money, women and pornography."

Father Anselm laughed, Martí stifled a giggle, but Uncle looked worried.

"Primo de Rivera came a cropper."

"The man was only a general," Father Silvestre said and closed his eyes.

"He's fleeing to France," father Anselm added.

France is the place to go, I thought. Martí and I looked at each other, I clicked my fingers, and we scrambled out to the street, forgetting to put out the candles. The sun was hot, the air was blowing crisp and lovely, and a scream came out of my chest.

"The king's a sinner! Hahaha!"

Martí was embarrassed, but I had fun. The king was the biggest sinner in the country, and no one ever bit him up for it. I wanted to know what was going to happen next.

So far, in April, we had elections, and the Republican Party won. The king also headed for France. People said that when he walked out of the royal palace, he cried.

I was so overwhelmed by the good news. I gathered a few friends, and we ran around the streets shouting.

"Long live the Republic and down with the clergy!"

At first, the people we met on the street looked astonished, the butcher came out of his shop to see us and laughed. We avoided the shops because we knew that the shopkeepers were Uncle's friends. At the corner of San Joan Square, an old lady crossed herself. It was a fun day. When I got back to Uncle's house, Aunt Teresa was waiting for me in rage.

"How could you do this to us?" she asked, she had been sweeping the stairs and hit me with the broom's handle. I ran to my room, but she followed me, hitting me in the back. To avoid the blows, I crawled under my bed, she pocked hard with the broom, but I grabbed the broom's stick by the top and managed to pull it off her hands. Poor Aunt Teresa she kneeled powerless by the bed crying and wiping her tears with her apron.

"Ungrateful child!" She cried. "God will punish you for such an affront to the church and us."

"I just wanted to express an opinion," I said.

"An opinion, who do you think you're?"

Next, I had to face Uncle's rage. But he was late Aunt Teresa sat on a chair saying the rosary. After the clock struck twelve, the key rattled, I heard Aunt getting up, the door opened, and I trembled.

“How come you’re so late?”

"I’ve been talking to the bishop.”

Uncle signed, and I was all ears.

“I fear for the future of the church," he said.

"Oh! But God is on our side."

"Yes, but the Republic is against God."

"Go to bed and don't worry about the Republic. In this city, people are with God."

“Well, we don’t know.”

Uncle sounded defeated, I heard doors opening and closing, and I felt sorry for my Uncle, but I wanted my freedom.

The following Sunday, Uncle's sermon was about different kinds of freedom.

"You must never confuse Freedom with libertinism," he said. The old ladies nodded.

"Real Freedom comes from God, and libertinism is brought to us by the devil. God has given us the freedom to choose between good and evil. But the merciful God chose Calvary to redeem our sins, and with his sacrifice, God showed the way to redeem ourselves and to do good for humanity."

"Oh, yes and stick in the mud," I said to myself.

Chapter 20

In the summer, we saw Marcel-lí again. He had grown very tall, and despite the sad stories of being in Solsona, he was fat. He spent his holidays in town with his uncle Robert. Sometimes, he came to our house, played with Brú, helped Father and searched around till he found something that needed mending.

"You see a wooden wedge between the handle of a small hoe and the socket, and it works again," he said.

"It's a pity, God has the opportunity to better yourself, but you're not able to take it," Father said.

But Marcel-lí found nothing in the church except oppression. On Sundays, Marcel-lí and his uncle went to help with Mass in all the churches in the town: St Aulalia's church, then St Joan and ended in the afternoon in St Francis. We thought it was cruel, but nothing could change his uncle's way of thinking.

"You can't allow religion to take over your life," Mother used to say, "The gospel is something well explained in church, but in real life, you have to work with your own hands and think with your head, you need common sense."

"You never say that in front of Father," I said.

"It would upset him. Men, priests, and politicians benefit too much from our ignorance," Mother said.

"What you're saying makes me sad," I said.

"Reality is hard, the lives of the poor are all toil and little joy, but we must thank God because we're in good health. We might think the rich are happy, but they are not. The men suffer from an incurable illness that comes from sin, and their offspring inherit the disease. " Mother said.

"Oh, God protects us from such misfortunes." I prayed.

The sky was darkening, and the rain was about to fall. I picked up the washing and took it indoors. Mother was sitting close to the balcony sewing a patch on Father's trousers. Father sat at the table. He had just finished eating his afternoon snack. I started to fold the washing when Brú began to bark. The barking stopped, and Josep's footsteps echoed through the house as he came up the stairs. The door was open, and he came in, holding a newspaper in his hand.

"Hello," he said.

"Good to see you here," Father said.

"Would you like something to eat?" Mother asked.

"No, thanks, I brought the paper; I wanted Father to read for himself President Azaña's speech," Josep stood next to Father and started to read the headlines.

"Spain is no longer Catholic," Josep shouted. Father closed his eyes as if in pain, and Josep dropped the paper on the table. Father picked it up and raised it to his eyes in silence. He stood up and with a sudden jerk flung the newspaper onto the fire. I had never seen Father so angry before. We watched the flames engulfing the paper. Father stabbed the paper with the poker stirring the pages.

"Even if this country is no longer Catholic, we are," Father vowed.

"At last, change is here," Josep said.

"It's only trouble," Father's voice became husky.

"I trust President Azaña," Josep said.

Father cleared his throat and took a deep breath staring at the black ashes left by the paper.

"He's out of touch with simple people like us," Father picked up a bread crumb from the table and ate it.

"He's a great intellectual," Josep added.

"If Azaña believes that he can tear the word of Christ out of my soul, he's a fool," Father said.

"Does it mean that God has abandoned us?" Mother asked.

"The old order is falling apart," Josep replied.

"Yes, but we'll have to live from our labour like always," Father added.

"Yes, but with secular education and union rights..." Josep said.

"I don't know what secular education means," Mother said, keeping her eyes on her sewing.

"Religion will no longer be pushed down people's throats," Josep replied assuming an air of superiority.

"Christianity is two thousand years old. It would be like pulling an old oak from its roots, it would leave behind such a hole that the soil would cave into it," Father said.

"It's the mind I'm talking about," Josep said.

"Bah! I've seen all this before," Father added.

"The church is crumbling, the rich trembling and we have nothing to lose, but our ignorance," Josep said.

"If the institutions of this country collapse, we'll go down with them," Father said.

"A new spirit is growing."

"Oh! A new spirit! Bha! The wind that blows in spring is nothing but the autumn wind

blowing the other way," Father hit the table with his right hand.

"Is not as simple as that," Josep said, pacing up and down.

"Good ideas, but there is no liberation from work," Father sneered.

"Oh! Lord," Mother said.

"Gosh, what a racket, the walls were not thick enough to contain the two voices. A few drops of rain hit the window, dimming the light. Mother put away her sewing. "It's too dark," she said.

I picked up my underwear from the clothes basket and went up to my room. I folded my knickers. I made them myself with white cotton and then crocheted the edges in different colours, red, yellow and green. I was tidying up my bra when a flash of lightning illuminated the window, and a peal of thunder shook the house. My knees buckled, and I screamed, running downstairs. I found my parents praying to Saint-Marc and the holy cross to stop the storm. Josep went to watch the rain pelting on the window panes. More lightning and more thunder.

"The tree is burning," Josep shouted.

"Come away from the balcony!" Father said.

"It's dangerous!" Mother said as she dragged Josep away by the hand".

We prayed till the rain stopped and we went outside to see the damage. A cloud of smoke had swallowed up the eucalyptus tree. Slowly the smoke dispersed, and I could only see the trunk. The wind had ripped off a branch and was dangling in the wind.

"Oh! God" I shrieked. The bed of long, Eucalyptus leaves creaked and wiggled still burning.

"I've never thought a tree could burn so quickly," Father said.

"It's only a piece of coal," Mother sighed.

"Is the tree dead?" Josep asked.

"I'm not sure, oaks are very resistant to fires, but this tree I don't know," Father replied.

It was so upsetting to see something so close to us destroyed in a flash. Brú whined scared behind the door, I rushed to cuddle him, and the warmth of his body made me feel alive again. Josep laughed, Father sighed, and Mother returned indoors.

Chapter 21

Mother was upset. Someone must have told her that I was seeing Oriól. I feared being left alone with her because she would start asking all sorts of questions about him, and I felt lost. We were both in front of the house, taking the washing from the washing line and folding it. She seized the opportunity to give yet another warning.

"We know nothing about this man," she said while putting a folded sheet into the basket.

"Well, he's Veronica's son," I replied and took another sheet from the washing line.

"Yes, I know but …"

"We enjoy talking," I said and gave Mother one end of the sheet and retreated a few steps. The sheet stretched, we joined the four edges and folded it into smaller parts.

"Everything begins with a talk," Mother said.

"He's such a kind man."

"Young men are charming, but in fact, they are like a fox stalking a chicken." Mother added.

"you don't know him," I said offended that she compared Orióol to a fox.

"They're all the same," Mother said, and she smoothed the pile of bed sheets, straightening the crumpled edges with her hand.

"Oriól is very polite," I added.

"He's smart," Mother said. The wind turned suddenly cold.

"You don't even know him and criticise him as if he were a menace," I said.

"Men are fickle," Mother said.

"Oh, Lord," I sighed, grabbed the linen basket by the handles and rushed indoors. I tidied up the clothes first and then the bed sheets slowly, waiting for the moment when Mother would go to milk the cows and I could escape to town to sell the milk. I longed for the quiet of the night and the calm of the old city streets.

By the end of the week, Father had run out of animal food. He harnessed the donkey and went into town. On his return, Mother and I went out to help unload the shopping from the donkey.

"Guess who I bumped into today?" Father asked.

"It's market day, you could have met someone from the village of Llinas," Mother smiled.

"I met Robert."

"Oh! Dear." I cringed. They were going to talk about Oriol. I grabbed a bag of carob pods and carried it indoors. But I couldn't help the temptation to listen to their conversation.

"Oriól's family came from the Basque country," Father said. "They used to live in Barcelona, but when brother got a job for a timber company up in the hills, they came to live in Berga. They say that Oriol's mother is a good woman, but Oriól is passionate about bullfighting, he swears and he calls himself an atheist." Father added.

Mother brought her hands to her head as if she were witnessing a murder.

"I don't believe any of that gossip."

"Rosana, we believe what we want to believe. Robert lives near his house, and he also works up in the hills not far from where Oriol works, so he must know something about him," Father said. My insides stirred madly. I rushed to the toilet and then to my room. I thought about what Father had said, and I decided that I would ask Oriól whether he believed in God or not.

But the night when I saw him again leaning on a wall and holding a cigarette between his fingers, I felt he was waiting for me. I was frightened, and I wanted to turn back and walk home through a different street. But I couldn't leave him there smoking and waiting till God knows when. It was beautiful to feel needed, and although I was sure he was a sinner, I walked up to him. We walked up the dark street together, and as soon as we reached the hill, he came closer and held my hand. Below the ruined castle I lost my virginity. The night was dark, and the bats were squealing and fluttering around as if they were the rightful dwellers of the stone ruins. First, we sat on the grass, and he kissed me, and I trembled. He seemed to enjoy my helplessness and kissed me again, and again.

"Is there something wrong with you, Rosana?" he asked.

"No," I mumbled.

"You seem in a daze," he said.

"I'm just cold, that's all," I replied, that was a reason for holding me tighter. Then, Oriól kissed me. I felt clumsy and foolish. I don't remember what happened except I felt something hard, warm coming inside me. It was painful, but a new feeling was stirring inside my body. After that day, my head was full of daydreams about Oriól. I felt transformed. I longed for the day when Oriól would be in town so I could be with him and feel alive.

The Cadi Mountain range was white with snow, and the sharp peak of La Nou seemed to connect the white earth with the blue sky. I just stood in the balcony gapping, feeling the sun in my skin with tears welling up, but feeling that Ernest was happy gathering insects not far from us, and hoped that one day Josep might take me to see him.

Chapter 22

April 1933

¡At last! The time had come to say Good-bey to the embarrassment I felt measuring cloth with the palm of my hand: Father taught me how to read and write. I no longer saw measuring tape like an idle snake lying on the table. It had a function. I also learned the intricate stitch to make buttonholes and made myself a new dress. The dress gave me a new sense of self and, on Sunday Mass, I felt equal to my friends Lola and Carmen who stood smiling at the church gate giving carnations to collect money for the church. My dream of being a dressmaker was one step nearer.

Uncle Roc, aunt María and Ramón moved to a house in the nearby village of Aviá. My friend Lola said that the house was like a mansion. The was a lion on the roof, and It had a cherry tree avenue and peacocks roaming around a topiary garden. I couldn't wait to see the place.

Dear God! Why did you let me fall into such a disgrace? In the morning, I woke up feeling sick. I rushed outside and hid behind the bushes at the back of the house. When the nausea was over, I thanked God for the healing power of the early morning breeze. Throughout the day, Mother said that I was living up in the clouds. At night, I couldn't sleep, and I prayed to God to come, pick me up and save me from my shame. However, since God was late, I thought about killing myself. But did I have the right to drag my unborn child to hell? I couldn't see a way out. In our village, when a girl felt pregnant, she expressed a sudden wish to become a nun, and if the baby's father refused to marry her, she disappeared into a convent. And the baby, dear God! What happened to the baby?

On the following Saturday, when I finished selling the milk, I saw Oriól leaning on the wall at the corner of the street. He was holding a cigarette between his fingers, and when he looked at me, I burst into tears. "I'm pregnant," I sobbed.

He brought the cigarette to his lips, inhaled, and I looked away.

"We'll get married," he said and took another draught of his cigarette.

His voice was reassuring. However, I still feared that he would disappear back to Barcelona. Together we walked up the hill, and before he left, he said he would come to the house and talk to Father. Surprisingly, he turned up to our house a week later. On hearing him, Father was taken aback and said nothing. But Mother said

"Oh, dear, we've no money!"

Father thought that we should wait till autumn so that we'd have saved some money. Oriól explained that he got a job near the church; he was going to work in the office of the republic, and it was essential for him to live close to his new job.

Oriól proved to be a good organiser because soon he had rented a house not far from the office and our wedding to take place.

Viviana made me a black wedding dress; in those days' brides wore black. Josep bought me a bouquet of artificial, white roses with silky ribbons and pretty pearls. As I walked up the church's steps, the guests praised my beauty, but I was dead worried about being sick. When the religious ceremony ended, I felt more at ease. We had a little party in the restaurant, and the sparkling wine tickled my nose and the day went by between fits of giggling and anguish. Josep drank too much and went blah blah blah about babies. The guests had walked a long way, and after they showered us with good wishes and warm congratulations left. Once we arrived at our new home, I kicked off my uncomfortable shoes and collapsed on the bed with an overwhelming feeling of release: so far, nothing had gone wrong. The house had electricity—a little click of the finger, and like magic, light everywhere. Messy candles and lost matches were a thing of the past.

The next day, I woke up with a husband close to me, with no cracks in the ceiling and no dark corners where the devil could hide. Thinking of it makes me laugh: the cooking pots were all shining new. And the set of glasses with painted daisies that were a gift from my friend looked pretty. I put the glasses on a shelf, and I couldn't stop looking at them. In this house, there was less washing, a little cleaning and only a few potatoes to peel. It was just beautiful! At dawn, I woke up to the bells ringing the Angelus and then the distant voice of cockerels from remote farmhouses.

I discovered that my husband was nothing like my Father when something went wrong, Father would say. "It's God's will." But Oriól would blame human sloppiness. He questioned everything. In the evening instead of saying the rosary, he read the newspaper. I began to see a circulation of daily newspapers called 'Solidad Obrera' and monthly magazines such as

‘Iniciales’. Those magazines appeared and disappeared because they way passed on from one worker to another.

However, so much reading, questioning and searching made Oriól restless. He not only knew what was going on in the city; he knew what happened in Barcelona, Madrid and beyond. At times, I resented so much reading so much thinking and such little talking. I feared that reading would damage his health; Don Quijote’s madness began reading too many books.

That summer Marcel-lí came to Berga, and he would come to the house, help Father and if Ramón happened to be there, they would have a little argument because Ramón didn’t understand why Marcel-lí was not making good use of his education. It was something none of us could understand. But we could see how happy he was at our house. He built stone towers, helped Father and most of all liked to repair broken things.

"See, it works again," I remember him saying while showing me a small hoe with a loose handle that he had fixed.

"A wooden wedge between the blade’s socket and the handle will keep it in place. It's like giving the tool a new life."

And as the summer ended a new life opened for Marcel-lí; his uncles from his Mother’s side came to visit him, and he went to live with them. They both lived near a town with a cotton Factory and Marcel-lí his first taste of freedom, but we didn’t see him till two years later.

The house felt empty, and times I walked up the hill just to see the cows grazing, the chickens roaming outdoors and Brú chasing butterflies. Mother’s favourite saying was that at the end of the day, nothing squares up and life goes on.

When my pregnancy began to show, I had to stay at home. I knew how upset Mother would be if she knew that I was pregnant. She used to say. “Men rob your dignity with the same ease and cunning as a wolf.

Our daughter arrived in the middle of a windy night. She had ash-brown healthy hair, sensitive amber eyes and perfect fingernails. Soon, her loud voice echoed around the house. Everyone could see she was not premature.

“It was a shotgun wedding.” Mother said.

I was Oriól angry, and I was mortified; he just didn’t understand that having such a healthy baby could upset anyone.

“Let people think whatever they fancy,” he said, “and let’s enjoy our wonderful baby.”

We gave the baby Mother’s name Filomena, but we called her Nina.

As Nina grew up, I began to think about how Marcel-lí was getting along with his mother’s uncles. Father said that he was helping his uncle with his busy knife sharpening. Repetitive and boring, I thought. He wasn’t going to stay there very long.

Chapter 23

1933

Two years had passed by before I saw Marcel-lí again. At first, I didn't recognise him. Nina was having a nap. He came upstairs with cautious steps as if he knew that Nina was sleeping.

"What a surprise!" I said.

He had grown tall and muscular. His beautiful hair fell gracefully over his blue eyes.

"I'm surprised as well to find you with a toddler."

Marcel-li sat at the table, and I gave him a glass of red wine with one of my new glasses. In his hand, the glass seemed to shrink almost out of sight, and I laughed. He sipped the wine and said.

"I got a job."

"That's good! Where?"

"In a garage. I am going to be an apprentice mechanic," he said and moved his long fingers over the table.

"Oh well, lucky you."

"We need freedom."

The word freedom was scary.

"And what're you going to do with so much freedom?"

He laughed, and I heard Nina crying. I went to pick her up thinking about what the word freedom meant. I carried her to the dining room. She was a picture of health and prettiness. He took her from my arms and said,

"Beautiful."

Nina clapped her hands, mumbling.

"Ta ta ta." She kicked her legs, and he put her on the floor.

"See what I mean? She needs her freedom."

I was glad because I thought that at last! He was going to be able to live the life he wanted. He gave a lecture on trade unions; his uncles were passionate members of the CNT, and there he learned about anarchism. Only getting rid of landlords and workers' collectives could end hunger. A little too topsy-turvy, I thought.

When Oriól got back, Nina picked Nina up. Oriól sat on a chair, and he sat Nina on his lap. I told him about Marcel-lí's visit and his crazy commitment to the CNT.

"Oh, well, the problem is that criminals undermine the country's institutions. To control the rise of the unions, ' King Alfonso instigated state terrorism. They paid killers to shoot trade union leaders and prominent workers. Local politicians are only the puppets of the king, added to that there are foreign criminal organizations that sabotage international companies such as Canadian Electricity."

"Sabotage," I asked.

"Yes, it means damage."

Nina began to kick her legs, and her Oriol put her on the floor. She began dancing and mumbling the song of the Giant of the pine tree around the table. A smile flitted past his face, and he lit a cigarette. He inhaled and puffed out the smoke away and said.

"As you can see, this kind of crime has left a deep hunger to destroy the corrupt order and create something honest, new and more transparent."

Oriól's head moved from right to left, and the smoke got trapped in the wall.

"I think that it's all pure idealism; the CNT, are powerless and besides they employ the same gangsters to kill their enemies as the employers' organizations do. I don't believe in fighting crime with more crime."

"What an embroilment." I picked Nina up and sat her on my lap. I was feeling shattered.

The old donkey died, and my parents moved to a house in the village. The house was a ghost because I had never seen it. It turned out that the mysterious house was at the back of the old 'Bull's Inn'. There was an entrance gate made of wooden planks. I pushed the gate and Nina, and I found ourselves in a narrow sunless, passage that ended with a wall and dung-hip. It was a real cul-de-sack. Brú barked and ran with joy, jumping up and down. Mother came out to welcome us. Inside, I smelled cows' fodder and fresh dung. We climbed a flight of wooden stairs and got straight into the dining room. On the right, there was the scullery and a dark corridor. At the other end is the fireplace, a balcony and a door leading to the loft. Nina ran to Father, who was sitting by the fire.

"Good to see you," he said.

Mother fetched a glass of milk for Nina.

"This house has electricity," Father said.

"But no water," Mother added. She showed me the rest of the house. I realised that Mother had a separate room from Father. The dark corridor had two more rooms the last one ricked of rancid pork fat, and it had a small window with a grid and a view to the landlord's garden. Nina chased the cat, but it ran away. We left the house with a deep feeling of loss. Brú hated the place because he followed us and refused to go back and we kept him.

Chapter 24

1936: The Beginning of the War

Fate had cheated me of my brothers; Ernest had been called up to do military service and was heading to Zaragoza. He came to say hello and goodbye, I barely recognised him; Ernest was tall and handsome. Nina didn't understand what was happening because she had never seen Ernest was dressed in his Sunday best and looked as if he was going to a wedding, but on second thoughts perhaps, he was going to a funeral. The next day I went to town to buy bread. As we walked, downhill Dandelion clocks flew up in the hot breeze.

"Look, Nina, look! You see those fluffy white balls we call them stars that fall from the sky." Nina giggled and walked, wobbling, down the path. On the main road, we walked under the shade of the plane trees. But it was still hot. When we arrived at the bakery, the door made an irritating, metallic clink that made me shiver. Inside, there was a wholesome smell of fresh bread. Anton, the baker, was behind the counter with a dusting of white flour all over his hat. He was talking to Pau, a worker from a dairy farm. Pau was a middle-aged man with an old, crumpled beret on his bald head, a squint on his left eye and the colour of his clothes had faded into a dirty grey. That day he smelled of cow fodder.

"Good morning," I said. Anton waved his right hand.

"The rich and powerful hate change," he said.

I realised that I had walked into the middle of a serious conversation.

"Too much to lose," Pau said.

"I'm afraid the social reforms that we've voted for will disappear," Anton said.

"Franco's troops had no proper boots," Pau added.

"We've to make do with espadrilles," Anton poked his foot from under the counter.

"But we're not fighting a war," Pau said.

"In a few days we will," Anton added.

It was scary everyone talked as if the war had already started. A cat poked its black and white head from the stairs. Nina stopped tugging at my skirt and began to chase him. Pau took a few cottage loaves and put them into a sack and then loaded the bag onto his shoulder and said,

"I still hope for a solution." The bell chinked again, and he left.

"Sorry Rosanna," said Anton, and he gave me a two-pound cottage loaf, "the country is in turmoil. "

I put the loaf into my basket, took Nina's hand and also left. As soon as we stepped into the hot sun, an army truck rattled past with every piece of iron shaking. What a fright! I left shaking. Nina wanted to cry but laughed.

Those days the road was a killer, one day we found a toad squashed to death. Another day a snake. It was upsetting for Nina and disgusting for me. But the trees seemed alive chirping cicadas. They reminded me of a children's story, and I told Nina the story of the cicada that spends all summer singing, and when the winter arrived, she had no food.

That evening Oriól was late, and I was worried because he hated overcooked vegetables. When he arrived, he picked Nina up, held her tightly in his arms and wouldn't let her go. Something must be wrong, I thought to myself.

"Franco is leading an uprising with Moroccan troops," he said.

"But we were fighting a war against Morocco not so long ago," I replied.

"Yes, Muslims rushing to the aid of Catholics. Incredible."

"And what's going to happen now?"

" It doesn't look good. The church and right-wing have come out in support of Franco's revolt."

"But the Republic will put it down."

"I hope so. It's worrying the German airforce is flying troops from Morocco."

I felt giddy. It was as if I were falling into a well. Nina began to cry. The next evening, Oriól reported that in the town, the civil guards fled, the rich cowered in their houses and the local republicans took to the streets. CNT members stole guns from the empty local police station and went out shouting their support for the Republic. The republican government was forced to armed students, workers and ordinary people to defend Fascism.

The road was busy with cars carrying young men to improvised training camps not far from the village. In a few days Franco took over Sevilla, and he was heading towards Madrid. Mussolini also sent troops and planes to support Franco. During the day, it was quiet, but in the evening, Oriól brought home the bad news. On the first page of the Vanguardia appeared pictures of German planes with the heading saying, 'No pasarán.' They shall not pass.

"They're arresting right-wing sympathisers and taking them to the Modelo prison," Oriól said with a worried face. "Some men went to the church, took out the furniture and made a bonfire in the middle of the square, and Marcel-lí was there."

"Oh, my God! What's going to happen to him. What can we do to help him?"

"Nothing," Oriól said, "If he's got no common sense, he'll have to face the consequences of his senseless actions."

Marcel-lí was only seventeen, and I cried; he was one of the first to enlist as a volunteer in the column Land and Freedom. Before leaving for Madrid, he came to say goodbye. When I saw him with a gun on his shoulder, I realised that war was real and very dangerous.

"From where did you get that gun Marcel-lí?" I asked.

"I stole it from the Civil Gard's quarters," he said with pride.

The gun in his hand scared me out of my wits. Nina rushed to his arms, he dropped the gun and picked her up.

"We must defend our freedom at all cost," he said.

Nina laughed.

"Without freedom we're nothing," Oriól added.

I sighed.

"To rush to the front like this, it's crazy, very crazy."

"There's no option."

"You'll be killed."

He lowered his voice.

"Oh, but you're always afraid, afraid of asserting yourself, afraid of life, afraid of the dark..."

The warmth of his voice made me feel like a child again.

Marcel-lí wouldn't hear my plea and said goodbye.

To our surprise, Nina responded as if she understood what he was saying.

"Bye-bye, see you soon," she said, and we both laughed.

I watched him walking down the hill with his stolen gun on his shoulder and remembered the time when his uncle Robert dragged him back to Solsona. But this time, no, Robert pushed him. He went out of his conviction.

I took Nina upstairs, and a sudden gust of hot wind carried a giant black beetle into the dining room, it fluttered around and settled on the table.

"Yuk!" Nina shrieked.

I squirmed, picked up the beetle with a towel and shook it out of the window.

"It's gone!" I said. Nina smiled.

I remembered Marcel-lí as a baby, and I cried and prayed for my brothers. I knew that no matter how much I loved them, my love was powerless.

Chapter 25

It was a sleepless night: Nina had a tummy ache. In the morning, after Oriól left, I went outside to wash her nappies.

I heard a truck's engine roaring between the plane trees. It pulled up by the church, Bru barked, and I saw several men jump out, shouting all at the same time. I rushed upstairs to look out of the window. Then I saw two men climbing onto the church roof and begin hammering: Oh God! I sighed they were demolishing the bell tower. A flock of startled sparrows twittered scared as they flew over the fields. From the house, I could only see the roof of the church, but I heard the sound of wood being dragged down the church's steps and crashing on the ground. The loud voices continued, but I only understood the word '... fascists. On seeing a thick column of smoke rising, I guessed they had made a bonfire with the pews. Behind the rising clouds of smoke, the sun faltered.

In the afternoon, silence had returned to the neighbourhood, the smoke had faded, and Nina woke up from her nap feeling better. I was curious about what had happened to the church. I took Nina and went to have a look. The air carried a smell of burnt pine. In front of the church steps, there was a pile of ash with the half-burnt pews and confessional door. Saint Bartomeu lay half-buried in ash, he had a broken mouth, and I could see the white clay inside his hollow mouth.

His unblinking eyes were staring up at a hazy sky. What once had been the belfry was now a scatter of rocks, and the bell was gone. I heard scary voices coming from the church, Nina was tugging at my skirt, and we left the dreadful scene.

Back home, I wasn't able to concentrate on anything. I nearly forgot to cook dinner. When Oriól got back, I heard his steps, but they were not his usual nimble steps, they sounded tired and heavy. When I asked him, who was responsible for the destruction of the church, he stared at the floor for some time before he said they were desperate young men full of grudges against the King and his friends in the church. 'Crazy' I thought to myself. Not everyone was a friend of the King. That evening I couldn't eat, and at night I couldn't sleep. I remembered my days up in the hills when I was scared of the wolf and the devil. I didn't know then that some people could be just as bad.

The following day, I dressed Nina in a pink dress and went to visit my parents. I found Father cleaning the cow's shed. When he saw us, he stopped his work.

"What's to become of us?" he asked. "No church to remind us that we are not beasts. If you treat people like animals, they will behave like animals."

"The Republic is building new schools all over the country," I said,

"Oriól believes that everything is for the better."

"I'm a Republican in favour of education, but not a communist that kills priests and burns churches. Once the mob is on the street, only brute force can control it," Father said.

Upstairs Mother gave Nina a few sweets, and she began to eat a sweet and walked down the corridor calling the cats with the sweet in her mouth. "Chin chin. chin."

The cats didn't show up. Nina began to take out the lid of the milk pot and put it back again. The irritating noise was unbearable.

"Shhh, Nina!" I said. We left early to avoid the scorching sun. But it was already hot outside, hot and clammy. There was no one to be seen in the butcher's shop, and the usual puddle of fresh blood had dried out but the place was ricked of sheep's piss and rotting hay. The dazzling sun shone on our faces, and we walked in a daze. On the main road, we walked under a refreshing tunnel of leaves. But there was the usual racket of cicadas buzzing, relentlessly. A bit further up, the old church stood in silence like an old grandmother who lost her memory and had no more stories to tell. Long before we arrived at our house Brú came to meet us jumping and whining. In front of the house, the ground was strewn with red-geranium petals that looked like drops of blood.

Ramón turned up to the house unexpectedly, crying. "Dear God, what's happened now?" I said to myself. He told us that the militia had turned up to the house armed with picks, hammers, and guns. They rushed to the end of the vegetable garden shouting 'down with the fascist' Then, they came to the house and began a frantic search till they found Uncle Dominic who had been hiding in the loft. To our dismay they took him away, Ramón hesitated, covered his face with both hands and then he said that they found the sculpture of Bernadette that stood near the water spring broken to pieces and dumped her on the field down below. And the following day our Uncle was found dead by the roadside with a bullet in his head. I sighed and held Nina close to my heart, feeling her body was the only thing that could offer a little comfort.

The church bell didn't toll for our uncle, and we didn't even have the consolation of having the funeral he deserved. We had to pray at home with a few relatives and friends. We were all left with a sense of injustice and devastated with grief.

Without the lively sound of the church bell ringing to prayer during the week or for Mass, Sunday mornings had become ordinary and rather dull. The feeling of joy that I experienced seeing people dressed in their colourful Sunday best walking at ease on their way to the church had faded into the past. Josep also went to fight in the war, and when he came to say goodbye, he was happy to go to defend his ideals. Ramón refused to fight, he was grieving for our dead uncle, and he went into hiding with other boys like him up in the hills near France. Everyone talked about ideals, and I didn't understand the meaning of the word. It sounded as if people were talking about a country that only existed in their minds.

Chapter 26

Nina's hair was growing in big curls falling over her blue eyes. I combed it back away from her face and tied a white, silky ribbon around her head.

"I want to see it!" Nina shouted.

Oriól lifted her to the mirror.

"See this pretty girl in the mirror?" He said, "She's Snow White."

Nina screamed in delight.

"Let's go out," Oriol took her by the hand, and they left.

I hung up my apron and followed them. Oriol drew a hop-scotch pattern with a long stick, and Nina began to hop and jump on one foot on the squares.

"One, two, three," Oriol counted.

The bow on Nina's hair was like a white dove trying to fly. Having reached square number four, she lost her step. We laughed loudly. Then we heard a truck roaring, Brú barked, and an army truck stopped. Oriól held his breath, and Nina stopped playing. A tall man jumped out, the truck's engine rattled again, and the man began to walk, energetically, towards our house. I had seen that gait before. Then, I saw the broad shoulders and a red and black CNT-FAI badge on his cap.

"Marcel-lí, is it you?" I asked.

"Yes, it's me," he smiled.

His face was thin, his hair too short, but his eyes still had the warmth that could pick him out in a crowd. Oriol stepped forwards to greet him with an open hand.

"It's good to see you," he said.

They both shook hands, and then Marcel-lí kissed me on the cheek. Nina picked up a stick from the pile of firewood and gave it to him. Marcel-lí bent down and took it from her hand.

"Thank you so much. I'm going to beat the Fascist with it."

"What a surprise," I said.

"We didn't expect to see you so soon," Oriol added.

Marcel-lí grinned, picked up Nina and with a quick movement, she pulled his cap off his head. Marcel-lí took the cap from her hand and put it over her small head.

"That's the prettiest republican fighter I've ever seen," Marcel-lí said.

Nina giggled.

"Pretty and clever," Oriól said.

"Gosh, she's as beautiful as you," Marcel-lí said, looking at me.

I wasn't used to hearing such flattery. We went upstairs, and Marcel-lí sat around the table. Marcel-lí was holding Nina on his lap. I served bread and dry sausage; the wine was already on the table.

Nina jumped out of Marcel-lí's lap and picked up a dolly, she kissed it and gave it to Marcel-li and said,

Kiss, kiss...it was all cheers and laughter. I went to the kitchen again to get a glass of milk for Nina. When I came back, the conversation had changed from baby talk to the harshness of war.

"We joined the 'Land and Freedom column and travelled from Madrid to the front. The next day I woke up to a burst of machine gunfire. Crawling on all fours, I rushed out and got into position to contain the attack. But my gunshots didn't hit anything." the gun was useless."

"How frustrating," Oriól said.

"After a few days, the casualties on our side were piling up," Marcel-lí added as he watched Nina slurping her milk.

"Please, Nina, be quiet," I said. Marcel-lí continued.

"We decided to retreat to Madrid, and on our way back we found the villages we had passed before under fascist air attack and burning.

"Bloody Fascists!" Oriol shouted. The furrow on his right eyebrow deepened.

How could God abandon his children so cruelly? I thought to myself.

Marcel-lí carried on with his account.

"In Madrid, we were led to the airport and the next day, the Health Minister Federica Montseny came to make a speech. 'There's no victory without casualties' she said, raising her first as she spoke to the microphone. 'Our Republic and our freedom must be defended at all cost.' She said.

"Young fighters sat on the ground holding their guns in their arms as if they were holding babies. Some walked away;

they had been under machine-gun fire for days; they had seen the casualties without gaining an inch of territory. 'Madam it's good to talk, but to win this war I need a proper machine gun!' I shouted.

"Good," Oriól said, "I'm with you for freedom, but I'm sceptical. I haven't got the faith. I'm not prepared to give up my life for any cause." Oriol said and touched Nina on her head, and then he looked at me. Sceptical, I wondered how many people in our village knew what the word meant.

Before leaving Marcel-lí kissed Nina, and he said he was going to Barcelona to learn how to operate a machine gun before returning to the front. We went out to see him off. Nina was holding her dolly close to her, and she raised the dolly's hand and made the doll wave goodbye. Marcel-lí laughed and shook hands with Oriól. Crying I kissed him goodbye.

"You are going to be killed," I said.

"Out there, there is a cause greater than ourselves," Marcel-lí said and waved goodbye."

"Oriól looked at me and said.

"He's still alive and well, so no need for tears." Oriól didn't understand my grief, and I was hurt and ignored him. My feelings were mine and mine alone. We walked back to the house in silence. I had the odd feeling that the war was going to be very long, bleak and painful.

Chapter 27

The swallows said goodbye. They gathered on the electricity lines across the city's High Street shitting on the passers-by. People said they flew to warmer climates across the sea. I wondered how many would survive and return to their old nest next April. The war had scattered my brothers all over the country, and I had no idea when I would see them again. A subdued look appeared in the village people. The old trudged along as if they were carrying a heavy load on their shoulders. The vivacious glitter on the young woman's eyes had shrivelled, and the only thing that could spark a little life into their faces was the sight of the postman. The first thing we used to ask as soon as we crossed paths with someone was whether they had any news from the front. But not many letters arrived, and the ones we received didn't say much. A letter would say that the fighters took a town and a few weeks later another said they lost it.

As the war intensified, sick and disabled fighters began to arrive back in the town. It was heartbreaking; young men would sit on cafeterias' chairs with their crotches resting on the walls looking at young girls passing by. I was afraid of talking to them. Afraid of what they would say would be too painful. Food became more and more expensive, especially bread, but in the market, we could buy potatoes, lentils, beans, and chickpeas.

Josep also came back home. While doing intensive training, he got short of breath, he tired quickly, and on one occasion, he collapsed.

Oriól's mother Veronica turned up to the house carrying a wicker basket with chicks. Bru barked excitedly, and I had to take the chicks inside the house.

"That's very thoughtful of you," I said.

"This kind of chick can lay eggs early," she said stroking Nina's hair. "Just at six months. Nina must have fresh eggs."

Nina looked at the huddle of chicks chirping, chirping calling for their mother.

Nina tried to imitate the chicks, "Piu, piupiu," Veronica took them out of the basket, and Nina wanted to pick one up, but the young chick ran away. I put out bread soaked in water for them. I imagined their mother calling and wondering where her little ones had gone.

"The city's streets are like a beehive of activity," Veronica said. "Young men from the whole region come to Berga to join the Land and Freedom column. They meet in the cultural centre to discuss politics until late in the night and later, they gather in the local bars to have a few drinks and then go around the streets all singing the International, and cries of Long live freedom."

I nodded. Nina picked up a chick.

"Put it down, he's scared," I called.

"Well, I'm going back because after carrying the chicks all that way I'm tired."

"I'm very grateful."

"Tell Oriól that I'll see him another day," Veronica said.

I remember clearly, the evening when the International Brigade arrived in the country. Oriól climbed upstairs with a new spring in his steps. Up in the dining room, he picked Nina up in his arms and said.

"It's fascinating people come from all over the world and risk their lives to help our Republic."

Gone was that subdued look that kept people's eyes fixed on the ground. A smile appeared on their faces.

Marcel-lí wrote a letter that read that with the help of the International Brigade, his column took Quinto. He fought the fascists all day, and in the evening a lorry brought food and water. Ernest ended up digging trenches in Huesca. He worked all day and from time to time hiding inside. Going out for a pee was risky; you could lose your life. Fighting the impertinent flies was as bad as fighting the enemy. After dark, the ambulance came to take the wounded to a makeshift hospital. They lost more fighters to pneumonia and severe throat infections than gun wounds. At home, to Father's chagrin, Josep kept going to the town to dance the tango.

Chrismas arrived, I would have loved to take Nina to the special midnight mass called the Cockerel Mass. In that mass, a shepherd brought a living lamb to Mass, and as the shepherd humbly knelt in front of silk-clad baby Jesus, the lamb's bleating echoed through the church. On Christmas day, I missed the lively children's voices going from house to house to sing carols.

The Festival of the Kings on the 5th of January, when the children come out in the streets with colourful paper lanterns to welcome the three Kings arriving on horseback, was also cancelled.

We lost Huesca. The region is so rocky and bare that it is impossible to defend it from Italian air attacks. But we didn't know the facts because the letters that came from Huesca contradicted each other. The papers didn't tell the truth.

A few days later, I saw the first refugees. Women and children were roaming over the fields, looking for something. When I reached the farm to buy milk, Eugeni said people were running away from bombed cities and picking weeds to eat. We had gone so far as to have to eat weeds.

In the evening, Oriól brought home the Vanguardia, and he read that a German ship loaded with guns for the fascist had been found on Spanish waters.

Chapter 29

I found my lively geraniums frozen stiff: I forgot to take them indoors. The faint winter sun didn't thaw the frozen ground.

In the village women wore home-knitted shawls and walked with their eyes fixed on the ground to avoid the puddles of mud that formed on the spots where the sun shone directly, melting the ice. Young children were well wrapped up in scarves, and they walked lead by their mother's hand. Sometimes, when villagers met, they would mutter a few words that no one could hear.

On our way to the butcher's, we met Lola. She seemed to have aged since the days we met in Viviana's house. She hid her face inside a scarf, but I recognised her dark eyes, but they had sunk into their sockets.

"Lola, how are you?" I asked.

"Well, Pau's been missing from his column," she replied.

"I'm sorry to hear that," I said."

"He's dead."

"He may be a prisoner," I added.

"They don't take prisoners," she cried, "The moors cut their throat or the fascists shoot them."

She searched for her hanky and dried her tears. I felt a strange feeling going up my legs and choking in my throat.

"How are your brothers?" she asked.

"We don't know anything at the moment," I replied.

"That's the worst," she sighed, "the anxiety of not knowing it's like a poison. A lot of what people say is just lies, in his last letter he sounded well and in good spirits, still believing that we could win, but we'll never win this war," she said.

"Oriól thinks that there will be an early truce and negotiations to bring peace," I said, trying to reassure her.

"We're going to pray for peace in Viviana's house next Sunday at three in the afternoon. It would be nice if you could come."

Nina tugged at my skirt and Lola left. Nina wanted to go and see her grandmother, but we had no time. I had a lot of washing to do, and in the dead of winter, it gets dark before you finish. In the evening, I told Oriol about the prayer.

"Hitler's sending more and more planes," he shouted, "If prayers could stop the Condor Legion bombing civilians, I would be praying all day."

I had never seen him so angry before. A few minutes passed before I dared to reply.

"Praying would not solve anything, but I want to show my friend that I share her grief," I said fearing another outburst of anger.

"Go if you like, but don't take Nina because she repeats everything she hears," he added. I hadn't thought about Nina. Oriól's lack of sympathy for other people's grief made me angry, then he said.

"I can't bear to see that sadness in your face. I'll take Nina for a walk behind the farmhouse, and you can go and pray with your old friends. I'll wait for you at your Mother's house."

The following Sunday, we ate a quick lunch, and then I rushed to tidy up the kitchen, and Oriól changed Nina's dress. The frost shone on the fields. The sparrows stepped between the furrows digging for seeds; the sky was so blue and the air so cold that my eyes filled with tears. On the main road, the plane trees heaved, creaked and the leaves rustled. Nina picked up a stick and dragged it along.

At the crossroads, Oriól took Nina down the road to the village while I walked to Viviana's house. I found the door open, but I still knocked. Viviana came out, "we have been waiting for you," she said. Up in the sewing room, the shutters were closed, and at the corner, the sewing machine stood in silence. Lola wore black and Carme blue. Lola stood and kissed me. Ana from the butcher shop also arrived. Viviana took out the rosary from her pocket, sat on her chair and began the first prayer. Dear God! How different it was from the happy days when we met there to sew a new dress.

We sat in a circle mumbling the prayer with little conviction and no confidence. After saying the rosary, Viviana put the beautiful white, glass rosary into her pocket. Lola and I left early, and poor Lola moved her head from side to side as she walked downstairs, she was taking each step as if she were treading on a freshly ploughed field. When we said goodbye, I feared she might faint. As I passed in front of the butcher's shop, I saw that the puddle of blood had frozen into a patch of solid red. Having reached my parents' narrow passage, I could only see a piece of sky. It was a real cul-de-sac. The dung pit by the door was full, and as I went into the ground floor, the cows lay peacefully but the place steamed with fresh dung. Upstairs I found Father sitting in front of the fire. Nina stood between his legs to keep her warm. I wished I were a child again. Oriól and Josep were having a discussion and Mother came out of her bedroom.

"The fascists have got to Aragon," Oriól said.

"Soon they will be here, and we'll have no food," Mother replied.

"No respect for the law or any kind of authority," Father mumbled.

"It was the right wing who had the idea that killing union leaders would solve the problems. They forgot that these days, people could read and the newspapers keep us informed about what goes on in the world," Josep said.

"The newspapers tell lies," Father replied, it's a crisis of faith."

"I've got plenty of faith," Josep snarled.

"Faith of the wrong kind," Father replied, shaking his head.

"What we need is freedom and knowledge to speculate, and put things to the test so that we can grow and be ourselves," Josep added, his face tensed in anger.

"Revenge killings, robberies and intimidation take place because of the breakdown of social order," Father snarled and hit the log on the fire with the poker igniting new flames that lit the corner.

"Years of injustice and the unpunished killing of anyone who dared to dissent was bound to result in people losing respect for the authorities," Josep said.

"This anarchy makes madmen feel like kings, and they believe they can do whatever they like," Father said and kept hitting the log.

"When we defend ourselves, we're seen as being morally wretched. It seems that killing is the exclusive extremist and the religious right." Josep hit the back of Father's chair. Mother was by the scullery crying.

Oriól decided we had to go home, and I was glad to get out of the discussion.

We walked back up the stony road by a single row of houses in silence. Nina surprised us, pointing at a column of smoke winding up the hill. People were making wood charcoal. At home, we only spoke a few essential words. Oriol spent a lot of time reading the paper, but when I asked what was happening in the world, he said he didn't know. Deep, inside myself, something was collapsing, I didn't know what it was, and I didn't have the words to say it. I felt isolated in my grief.

In February our troops recaptured the city of Teruel. The small victory made us forget the dead, and it raised our expectations. However, the celebration didn't last long because we lost the city only a few weeks later. In March the bombings were nearer. In the fields, the corn was, and life went on. But I couldn't stop thinking about the people who wouldn't be able to smell the maiden pinks.

Chapter 30

Spring 1938

In March the Italian air force bombed Barcelona. A bombe fell on a church killing the women and children who were sheltering there. I was confused. God is merciful, but I couldn't understand how God could abandon his children in such a cruel way. I was too angry to pray, and I felt as if my child had died. I thought about the mothers who might have survived the bombings but lost their children. I sat on a chair outside because it was comforting to hear the birds singing. I ignored Nina, and she threw her doll on the ground and cried, for she knew that I was there, but half dead.

Easter Sunday was a day with no singing, no celebrations, and no resurrection. I was afraid of going to town because I could see more and more people dressed in black: girls wore dead cotton dresses, and boys wore a black badge on the sleeve. Greif was heard in women's mumbling voices and seen in children's eyes. Life was no more than a precarious existence, and anything could happen at any moment. Our only defence was the lie, we lied to ourselves and each other, pretending that we were stronger than we were, being cheerful for others and then collapsing into tears as soon as we were on our own. And the lie was growing every day. It was like a ghost leading us straight to our destruction.

In the evenings I waited for Oriól's return, but I feared what the paper was going to report about the front. We were going to win the war, but no one could say how. I saw pictures of the trail of destruction left by the bombing of cities in the newspaper. Random air attacks followed, aiming to kill civilians and cause panic among the population.

"The bloody bastards," Oriól shouted.

"The monsters are killing women and children, and they call themselves the True Spain; the God-loving and God-fearing Spain, but they're capable of killing innocent children. And on Saturday they will queue up to confess, and on Sunday they will receive Holy Communion, and God will forgive them."

"Whether God will forgive them or not, it's not for us to decide," I said.

"It's not for us to decide, but it is for us to question?" he replied.

"I'm not able to remember how to say the rosary let alone to question God's intentions," I added.

"We have the right to think for ourselves and to question everything. Have you heard that?"

"Yes, I have, but I was taught to have respect for others," I replied.

"I'm asking you to think for yourself, and you give the same old reply. I heard that, far too many times. I want to see you thinking with your mind. "

A domestic war had broken out. Oriól wasn't used to being answered back. It was impossible to agree on anything at all.

We stopped being able to understand each other's points of view. Our anger poisoned our nights together. He expected me to believe everything he said, but I didn't anymore. I hated my weakness and my lack of courage.

It was a time of sudden rains and sporadic storms. Hailstones as big as eggs fell hitting the animals hard, sometimes on the head and after the storm, we could see young dead birds laying stiff at the edge of the fields or on the path.

German planes bombarded the town of Guernica while smaller Italian fighter planes machine-gunned the terrified population as they tried to run for shelter in the forest. The streets became heaps of smouldering debris. Clouds of purple smoke covered the sky. Survivors carried their belongings to safety. Wounded people lay on mattresses on the roadside, waiting for ambulances to take them to the nearest hospital.

"See what I was telling you, killing the people is not enough. They aim to destroy not only us but our culture as well. They want to see our history turned to a pile of rubble."

A strange feeling paralysed my legs, and my thoughts rushed around my head: The future was dead. That night I felt Oriól's hand as I dreamt about the city of Guernica, I saw black piles of rubble and an empty shoe lying around. A barefoot stuck out of the ruins. Then black spots began to stir from the purple sky, flocks of swallows flew around trying to return to their old nest, but the swallows flew around and around over the ruins twittering in despair because they couldn't find their old nest.

Chapter 31

October 1938

The swallows had gone away, but flocks of sparrows flew twittering searching for food on the fields. Franco said that the International Brigade impeded achieving a truce and negotiating peace. And the country believed him. We saw the pictures of proud young, foreign men from all over the world marching along the streets of Barcelona before going back home in the papers. We were to have peace, our men would come home, and there would be food on the table. But as soon as the International Brigade left, the country endured more and more bombings.

Boys scattered seeds over the stubble, and when the sparrows came to feed the boys trapped them with nets. Sparrows were a delicacy, but it took too long to pluck them. The feeling of holding that warm, soft, lifeless little body between my fingers made me shiver.

Nina had heard the butcher's boys saying that from Noet's hill, you could see fantastic views of the city of Berga and lots of high mountain peaks and she wanted to go. I thought it was too steep for Nina to walk up there. But Oriól said it would be fine. He would carry Nina on his back when she got tired.

The trip began on a Saturday afternoon we started the walk. In front of the closed church, we scared a tabby cat sleeping on the steps, and it ran into the cemetery. Nina looked sad because she loved cats. Climbing up the hill proved tough; the track was narrow and slippery. My heart was beating fast, but as the view expanded my spirit went up because I was leaving behind the drudgery of everyday life and felt was getting close to heaven. Halfway up, Oriól turned around and said.

"Look, Nina, our house is getting smaller, and by the time we get back we won't be able to get in."

"Don't believe that," I said, "Your father is a joker." Overgrown brambles trailed here and there, and clusters of gorse yellow blooms spread over the hillside. At the hilltop, it was all fresh breeze pure sunlight. The space in front of my eyes awoke in me an immense feeling of freedom. There was the world I had left behind: the house on the hill, the path I trod so painfully to go and sell milk. Built at the foothill the city of Berga was a landscape of roofs zigzagging and overlapping over each other with odd windows and wooden balconies. Oriól pointed to a few places to Nina, and she was delighted to see so many houses clustered together and the football pitch on edge. Suddenly we heard the grating sound of an iron pick hitting a rock.

"What can that be?" Oriól said. We walked in that direction, and we saw

republican soldiers were digging a grave-like hole in the hillside.

"It's a trench," Oriól said, as we approached them.

"A trench, a trench," Nina chirped.

"Hello, are they here already?" Oriól asked.

"Not yet," replied the oldest soldier.

"But a little nearer," added the youngest grinning.

"Without the International Brigades who knows what's going to happen," the

old soldier said.

"It's such a lovely day," I said.

"Yep, it's a pity there's a war on," the young soldier said.

The old soldier picked a sprig of late-flowering rosemary and gave it to Nina.

"Rosemary is the herb of remembrance, and it's for the blue-eyed princess," he said. Nina smiled shyly.

A few pale blue flowers remained in the sprig. Nina smelled the pungent smell and gave it to me. We left the men to continue their hard work and walked to the other end of the hill. We could see small houses scattered around and the grazing cows below seemed to be only tiny dots. Far in the background, we could see the sharp mountain peak of the Nou. Oriól plucked a few box leaves and chewed the bitter leaves the way we used to do in the hills to quench our thirst.

"It's time we started to walk back," I said.

"Yes, Nina must be tired," he replied.

"I'm not tired," Nina said, "I like it here."

The way down was easy but dangerous; loose stones slipped beneath our feet and I was afraid of falling. When we got as far as the farmhouse, we found Florencia shaking a bucket of corn. Chickens began to appear running from the nearby fields. She scattered handfuls of corn in small quantities, keeping some corn for the last ones.

"They're digging a trench up the hill," Oriól said.

"We didn't see anyone going up," Florencia replied.

"Oh, well, both sides keep the truth hidden from us. It's unbearable." Oriól said.

"That awkward feeling of floating in a sea of lies drives me crazy."

We got the milk and went back home.

One day Oriól brought home a radio. When I saw the mysterious wooden box, I remembered that the Fascists considered people who had radios to be traitors. But Oriól said that he needed to know if or when it was the time for him to run away. I was terrified. Every evening before going to bed Oriól got out the radio and plugged it in. A storm of sounds hit straight at my head. I felt a current of fear running down my spine. I thought the odd box was going to explode. Oriól would start to turn the knob around till he found Radio Catalonia. The bombing of Barcelona left the city's buildings guttered. Many people lost their lives, and there was a frantic effort to dig the wounded from the piles of rubble.

German planes called 'swallows' dropped incendiary bombs, and the smaller Italian ones killed the people. I couldn't comprehend how such destructive things could be called swallows. Terror gripped our lives. I just waited to hear what atrocities the radio was going to report. Seeing pictures in the papers of mothers kneeling in front of their dead children made me ill. I lost my appetite, my breasts sagged, and I felt ugly.

Every Thursday, the pork butcher slaughtered a pig, and by the afternoon, the meat was ready to sell. But few people could afford to buy anything except pork fat. Oriól earned 50 pesetas a week, and bread alone cost 17 pesetas a loaf, so we had to be very careful. I dressed Nina in her blue dress and white jumper. I combed her beautiful curls and tied a blue bow over her head. I didn't bother with my clothes and just wore an old skirt and espadrilles. I took the wicker basket to carry the bacon and the milk pot because on our way back we were going to buy milk from the farmhouse below the hill.

We found Mother, who never wasted a single moment, on the balcony hanging out the washing.

"Hello, Grandma! Nina called as we opened the wooden gate. Inside the house, the cows lay on fresh hay, but the first cow stood up, raised her tail and crapped.

"Caca, big caca, "Nina laughed.

Josep was at home; he was sitting resting his hands on the table.

"Hello, Nina," Josep said, "Your eyes are so beautiful like Dahlia's."

"Dahlia, who is she?" I asked.

"My new girlfriend," Josep replied.

"What happened to the old one?" Father asked.

"She lost interest," Josep replied.

"She must have got tired of dancing the tango up and down the dance hall and never getting anywhere," Father said, got up and sat by the fire.

"There's a war, and I've no money," Josep said, making a few tango steps up and down the dining room. Mother blocked his way and pushed him to the chair that Father just left.

"Show a little respect," she said.

Josep pursed his lips and tensed his body. Father started to stir the coals with the poker.

"I need money for guano you waste it in the dance hall," Father said.

"My life is out of kilter, and dancing is my only comfort."

Our lives were out of kilter. In the street where I used to meet friends carrying water or washing, now they were carrying water and shouting at their children. The rag and bone trader came to buy rabbit hides and would wander around shouting for skins, but no one had any to sell.

Chapter 32

A month later, I went home to see whether they had any news from the men on the front. Mother was in the street her dark figure was swaying as she walked carrying two buckets of water from the drinking tap in the cattle trough. Nina ran ahead to kiss her. Mother's knobby fingers curled holding the bucket's handle like the branches of an old oak. I took the buckets and carried the water for her. The sun was shining high up on the red brick wall of the narrow passage. Upstairs, Father was sitting by the fire. Mother gave Nina a cup of milk, and then we heard a mewling of kittens coming from the last room.

"Their mother goes away hunting and leaves them without milk," Mother sighed.

"Kittens, kittens," Nina screamed. I went to put the empty cup into the sink when the door at the end of the dark corridor opened by itself; three kittens came out and ran along towards the hall. The last kitten was shy and lagged in hesitation. Mother put out a saucer of milk on the floor for them. Then the door they came out from opened wide and a thin man with a long beard came out. He started to smile, but instead, a deep cough came out of his throat.

"Ernest!" I cried.

"We agreed that you wouldn't come out," Father said.

"I was getting bored," Ernest said in a faint voice.

"Children can't stop telling people everything they see. That's how they discover deserters," Mother said. It was sad to see her so distressed.

I hugged Ernest. He was so thin I only felt his bones.

"It's so lovely to see you again," I cried.

"I feared this moment would never come. Mind you. I'm not out of danger yet," Ernest said. Nina hid her face behind my back.

"There was no point in fighting any longer," he replied, "We're losing, and losing badly. The lieutenant was forcing us to fight at gunpoint, men falling one after the other. The war was no longer fair. I ran and ran for several days, eating nothing, only drinking stream water that I found on my way."

"But they'll arrest you for desertion," I said.

"I have removed two of the iron bars from the window so if they come. I'll jump into the landlord's garden. The landlord told me that I could hide in his house," Ernest explained, and he coughed again.

"And what do you do to pass the time?" I asked.

"During the day I read and, in the night, I go up to the loft. From the balcony upstairs, I watch the cycles of the moon and the stars. I also have fun watching the cats chasing each other on the roof in front of the house. There is a new tom cat that sends all the females running." Ernest laughed, and his cough started up again.

"I told you to stay in bed," Mother told him.

"What did the doctor say?" I asked.

"We haven't called him," said Mother.

"If people saw the doctor coming, they would suspect that someone is hiding here," Father added.

Ernest coughed again. "Go back to bed," Mother told him. Ernest and his trail of kittens walked along the corridor, and he closed the door, waving goodbye.

"Nina, you must never tell anyone that you saw Uncle Ernest in grandmother's house," I said.

"No, I will never say anything," Nina replied, and her eyes remained fixed on the closed door at the end of the dark corridor.

I was worried about Nina telling people that Ernest was home. In the evening, when Nina was asleep, I told Oriól that I met Ernest because he was hiding at my parent's home, and when he knew that Nina saw him, he was furious.

"Having to teach Nina to lie is not right, not right at all," he said and looked away.

"Nina is a sensible girl," I replied.

"Yes, she is, but she's also very young, too young to have to deal with such situations.

"I don't think that people will ask such a small girl where her uncle is," I said, trying to calm him."

"I hope not, but I hate the idea that we'll have to learn to tell lies for the rest of our lives" Oriól added. "We'll have to say what they want us to say and say it in their language. It's the imperialist mentality: they see themselves as a model that we'll have to imitate, and if you're not happy, you must be potty or subversive," Oriól grinned. Seeing his moods go up and down so suddenly worried me more and more.

Chapter 33

1938

In the streets of Berga, more women wore black. They walked into the market, holding their children's hands. They wandered from one stall to the next asking for prices and moving away without buying anything at all. They tightened their grip on their children's hands as if in fear, that the children might be blown away by a gust of wind. Letters from the front stopped arriving, and families were left wondering whether their sons, husbands or fathers were dead or alive. It took a long time before we learned what was going on on the front line.

Oriól found Brú dead on the road. He had been run over by mad republican drivers. We didn't grieve much for him because we had no food, but without him barking the house felt dead. In Barcelona, the violence in the rearguard got worse, after two Italian Anarchists appeared dead in the gutter, the situation got much worse. A fight between the CNT and communists broke out. CNT members were tortured and put to death. People didn't know what was happening and when Oriól listened to the news, he got furious.

"I don't know what they're doing; when they have a gun in their hand, they start shooting each other, idiots!" Oriól shouted at the radio. I felt we were all walking blindingly into a dead end, but I kept silent so as not to upset Oriól.

Days went by, and the Militia did not come to arrest Oriól, they were too busy fighting the enemy in the front. We heard on the radio that the Fascist troops were concentrating on the west side of the river Ebro in Aragon. The republican forces were on the east. They were waiting to see who would make the first step to cross the river and launch the final attack. The people were still hoping for a truce and peace, but Franco said.

"I don't want peace; I want a victory."

I didn't imagine the river as a river but as a terrible monster feeding on our young people. It was everyone's nightmare.

"We're losing on the Ebro," he said as he came through the front door.

"And what do you think is going to happen?" I asked.

"Once they have crossed the river, our forces won't be able to stop them," Oriol replied collapsing on a chair.

"But then our lives will be the same," I said.

"Our lives will not be the same; we are going to lose our language, culture, and identity. We'll have to sing the Fascist national anthem, speak their language and live on our knees."

I didn't know what identity meant; I thought it meant something inside us. I didn't want to think about such complicated things because it made me very depressed. Nina started school, and every time we walked from the house to the main road and then under the trees. Lots of army cars passed, and I got frightened.

More refugees from the bombings of their cities arrived in the village. I knew when they were refugees because they walked with their eyes on the ground, their hands close to their hearts and dressed in black. People talked behind their backs telling their stories to each other: she lost her husband or son; she was beaten, raped and humiliated in front of her children.

Hitler had sent new warplanes that were light and swift. Those planes could swoop, drop bombs and rise again. With those planes, the fascists destroyed whole towns and killed thousands of people as they were trying to escape. The Republic made another call-up, and some of the most recent recruits were only seventeen. After a few days of training and off they went to defend our homeland, our dear language, and freedom. Sadly, their young lives didn't buy our freedom; after days of intense fighting, the Ebro was lost. Our young soldiers were thrown into the river, or their dead bodies were sprayed with petrol and burned. But some managed to escape, and they walked for days without food during the night until they reached home. All we could hear on the radio was.

"No pasarán!"

"But they're passing," Oriól shouted back.

"Put the radio off! You're making yourself ill," I said. But he followed his mind, and he would never listen.

The frost took us by surprise and with no food in our larders; if you had plenty of silver to buy it in the black market, you could have bought anything you wanted.

Chapter 35

The year 1939 end of the war

It was Candlemas when we heard gunfire for the first time; the Fascists had reached the nearby village of Aviá.

"It's time to run," Oriól said. I felt a sharp pain tummy and warm blood began to flow between my legs. I rushed to the toilet and sat there until I had gathered all my strength to face the future. Oriól took the rucksack and filled it with salted pork fat and bread. I piled up a few clothes wrapped them up in a backpack and left it ready for the evening. The shooting continued throughout the day, but in the evening it stopped. When it was dark enough, Oriól took the rucksack and a bag of clothes for Nina. Oriól closed the door quietly, and we walked down towards my parent's house. The pale light of a waning moon filtered through the bare trees and formed a crisscross pattern of darkness and twinkling stars.

"Why are we going out in the night?" Nina asked.

"Your Father is going on a long trip, and we're going to spend a few days in grandma's house," I replied.

"You'll be able to play with the kittens," Oriól added.

A barn owl screeched, and I envied its ability to blend with the darkness.

At home, we found Ernest with his rucksack ready to start the long trek across the Pyrenees to France. Mother was crying, and Father was praying. Oriól settled Nina in Ernest's bed, he kissed us, took his rucksack and rushed down the stairs. Ernest followed him, and I went to see them off to the door. I heard the familiar footsteps fading into the unknown. I went back and collapsed next to Father sobbing and wanting to be sick, but I had nothing in my stomach. We prayed until the early hours of the morning. Josep hid from the retreating army in the mountains.

The next morning Nuria called from her window to say that the Republican fighters were retreating and people went to see them. We went to see our army marching past along the road. Longbeards hid their faces, and their eyes had sunk in their long hair straggling under dusty caps, torn uniforms, espadrilles falling to pieces, feet bleeding. A soldier stopped to pick up something from the floor, and the officer hit him with the butt of his gun. Nina cried, and then we all cried. I felt as if I had swallowed a stone.

We prayed for a long time Nina, and I was sorry that I had taken to see such a sight. In the night I heard the sound of mice scurrying across the loft while the cat grabbed it; the mouse squeaked as it was being eaten alive.

I woke up the next morning into a world to the terrifying sounds of planes roaring over Noet's Hill. Lola came to the house. The first bomb exploded into a ball of fire. She shouted that we had to seek shelter in the sheep's yard because the walls there were thicker. My parents decided to stay put because they had to take care of the cows. The first bomb explodedfar away, but the second fell on the hill. Another plane appeared and then another. The planes were flying in circles dropping bombs on the hill. Each bomb started a fire. Nina screamed and then kicked. I had to carry Nina to the butcher's sheep yard. Instead of sheep, we found our friends and neighbours huddled together. Ana and his two boys, Edmond and Lluis, looked pale and Ana shivered. The hay on the floor was soggy and reeked of sheep's urine, and droppings were scattered all over the yard. I held Nina close to my tummy as if I could keep her safe inside myself. Lola looked at me and then she said.

"The Moors, I'm terrified of the Moors."

"Why're people so scared of the Moors?" Lluis asked.

"They steal watches," Ana replied.

"But we don't have any," Edmond said.

"You won't understand it," Ana replied.

Nina stopped crying, as we listened to the roaring of a car pulling up in front of the yard. We were a shivering mass of bodies holding together, ready to meet our worse fate. The door shook, and a soldier appeared. I had never seen such good boots. The tall soldier stood there with a musket in his hand.

"Why are you so scared," he said in perfect Spanish. No one replied, "Go home, you 've nothing to fear."

"Where's the Moors? Lluis asked.

"Shut up" Ana replied. The soldier smiled.

"The Moors won't come here," The soldier said.

I sighed, and Lola sneezed. Ana wiped a tear, and my body was trembling. I had been afraid for so long that the fear wouldn't leave me. Ana was the first to take her boys back home. I also walked down the road to the roar of planes flying over the hill bombing the trench. I was carrying Nina in my arms, and the hill was burning. I was sick. At home, the cows were still there chewing their cud. Upstairs, Father was sitting by the fire and Mother at his side, peeling potatoes for the evening meal. Mother gave Nina some milk, and I went straight into bed. About one o'clock the next morning, I woke to the caterwauling and growling of cats matting on the roof in front. The following day, I didn't have the strength to go out and see the sadness that had engulfed the whole village. We had to forget the Republic and remember to call the Fascist Nationalists.

The following Sunday morning, we heard the bells ringing again. It was the call to Sunday Mass. Father had a bad cough and Mother stayed home to look after the cows. Since it was cold, I left Nina in bed to keep warm. The church was cold, and it smelled of old mildew and fresh pine. The parishioners arrived with a whiff of Eau de Cologne. They walked down the aisle. The men sat to the left, and the women to the right. My friends Lola and Carmen did show up. It was sad. I sat with my eyes fixed on the restored San Bartolomeo. He stood on his plinth with a devil writhing under his foot. According to the legend he exorcised a devil from a man thus freeing him from evil. But the saint never came to help us. My mind wandered around. The mass felt like a funeral. But not an ordinary one. One for the death of our people, our language and our way of life. After mass, people gathered outside the church as they used to do before the war broke out. I could see a deep pain in peoples' faces and how they struggled to suppress it. I went to greet Eugeni and Francisca.

"You have no idea what we have been through," Francisca said.

"I found a dying soldier at the edge of a field. I was so scared. I called my husband, and we tried helping him, but he couldn't move. He gave us his parents' address in Barcelona, his wristwatch and his pocket knife and then died. We buried him in the night and posted his belongings to the family."

"Please God keep him in heaven," Eugeni said.

Francisca burst into tears and did the same. Slowly the congregation dispersed some people went up the hill, down the valley and others towards the village of Aviá. A few days later the Nationalists celebrated their victory with a big party in the restaurant. But we had nothing to celebrate and stayed home. Ramón returned home in a state of severe malnutrition. Nuria's husband also reappeared in the middle of the night just to die the following morning. Children returned to school, and I went back to an empty house. It was time to cry with grief and hunger.

Chapter 36

Alicante 1939

In Quinto, the column's commissioner came in the middle of the morning and told us that the war had ended and there was no need to fight anymore. He said we had to wait till dark. An army truck would come to pick us up. Then we would travel overnight to Alicante harbour. There, we would board a ship and sail to Algeria. But after the long night's journey singing 'Ay Carmela' in a crowded truck moving from side to side, and falling on each other. Finally, we arrived at a city gutted by fire.

"Fuck!" Colom said, "The bastards have bombed the city."

The truck shook and rattled like mad over a maze of smouldering streets. When finally we reached the West Pier, we found it chocked with refugees. My friend Colom looked at the crowd, swearing in a rage.

"Fuck, fuck! Look at all this!"

A woman in a black scarf looked at us and said.

"An English ship left last night. It was so full of refugees that we couldn't get on."

"Shit! And how do we get out of here," I asked.

"We'll see," Colom added.

Children were crying, grownups coughing and waves crashing in the breakwater. More refugees arrived wrapped up in blankets and loaded with a few belongings. Some were ex-combatants, survivors of the Ebro battle. Others were old men women and children, of all ages, that had managed to escape from the rapes and killings perpetrated by the Moroccan army. A tottering old man cried and coughed as he tried to mumble a few words. But we could only understand one word. "Family, family," he said. He must have lost his family, I thought. After a while, we saw his exhausted body laying under a blanket—the night before it had rained. They made a bonfire with pieces of wood trying to keep warm. Then there was a scream; fuck, a soldier jumped into the sea. The crowd watched in despair.

Three days went by, and we were still waiting. In front of us, the sky was reddening. The city's building was still smouldering. The ancient castle of Santa Barbara stood under a cloud of smoke with solid impassivity. I managed a little sleep. In my dreams, I was still fighting in Quinto. I could hear my friends swearing mad at every explosion and then, jumping in a celebration; we had survived.

Some ex-combatants paced up and down the pier looking nervously out to sea. But since we didn't know where our next meal was going to come from, I thought it was better to keep quiet and conserve energy. My limbs were numb with inactivity, and my eyes remained fixed on the broken orange lines shifting on the waves. Any little shadow was a ship, as it approached the ship because roller its journey ended with a mighty splash on the breakwater.

The next morning among the cries, voices and coughs I heard a man saying that he had heard that the city was under Fascist control—two simultaneous shots. Two ex-combatants shot each other at the same time. More cries, more sobs, then, I heard the bells ringing, and I felt utterly trapped. The crowd screamed again as another soldier jumped into the sea.

"A ship! I see a ship!" Colom shouted.

A grey line appeared on the horizon and then another and another. Refugees cheered. But as the ships approached...horror and dismay: We saw the red and gold Fascist flags flying in the air. The ships were minelayers belonging to Franco's army. For three days, we had been waiting for that bloody moment. Then the green uniforms of the Italian Littorio Division streamed down from the Avenida de Alfonso el Sabio. They swiftly closed in on the republicans sheltering in the West Quay. They rounded them up into a mass of emaciated humanity. Some republican fighters tried to resist and to escape. Then, General Gambara himself appeared dressed in full Fascist garb: a flat-topped hat over a square face, long nose.

"Look at him," Colom said, "short legs, long boots, baggy pants."

"Full of bollocks," I added.

"Don't let the criminals escape," Gambara shouted with a clownish smile.

"Bloody fanatics," Colom shouted.

The Moorish troops took us by surprise. They had filtered through the back streets and had begun to disarm the baffled republican soldiers.

"Hand in your guns!" Gambara said in Spanish but Italian accent. They took the men and left the women and children.

"Take them to the cinemas," Gambara shouted.

Other ex-combatants were forced at gunpoint up the hill to Santa Barbara Castle. More gunshots. The castle was hovering in clouds of smoke. With drunken footsteps, we tottered along. We were frog marched to the station and packed into wagons scattered with animal dung. A soldier suffocated to death and at the next stop, he was dumped on the station platform.

Late that night, we arrived in the concentration camps of Albateras. Others went to Los Almendros. We slept under a canopy of palm fronds till the next day when they set up tents for us: no sanitation and little drinking water. The Almendros' prisoners were more fortunate than us because they ate the young almonds, the leaves and the bark of the almond grove. We couldn't eat either the palm bark and the fronts were out of reach.

Chapter 37

It was dawn, in the village of La Valldan. I woke up to the bells ringing the Angelus, but I only could mumble a few words and the prayer faded in my mouth. The night before we ate the last handful of lentils. Without Oriól's salary, I didn't know what was to become of us. When I took Nina to school the morning was cold, the stubble was rotting on the fields, and the sky was so blue that tears welled up in my eyes. When we walked past the house that was once the office for the Republic, all the windows remained closed. The plane trees were still bare, and the road was a tunnel lined with skeletal shadows that moved here and there. Nina stepped on a shadow, but as soon her little foot touch it vanished just reappeared again. Nina laughed and jumped on the next shadow that seemed to fall from the trees, but I felt dizzy.

While Nina was at school, I went to beg for food. First, I went to San Llorenç farmhouse because I knew the people. It was too early for potatoes, the hens didn't lay eggs, and the fruit trees were just beginning to blossom, but they were able to give me a few leaves of winter cabbage and a handful of dry beans.

Nina told me that at school they had hung a long cloth that was a Spanish flag on the wall and above the flag a picture of a man called Generalissimo Franco. He had saved our country. Nina sang the Cara el Sol as I walked in silence. I looked at the trees and thought that those trees must be tired of always standing up.

On victory day, I went to my parents' house, hoping to get a little milk. Lola was walking up the street carrying two buckets of wet washing. She wore a grey-cotton dress and her body sagged under the weight of the buckets. She stopped, left the buckets on the ground, and she began to talk.

"Have you heard the latest news? She asked.

I nodded.

“The Vanguardia said that Barcelona dawned white. It makes me sick of the city’s streets streaming with Moorish soldiers dressed in white. White sheets were hanging from balconies; fascists marching victoriously; white flags waving, killers rapists and robbers celebrated as heroes. I want to kill myself.

"I sighed."

"And do you know what they do on those morbid concentration camps? Groups of Falangist travel from all over the country to take the prisoner back to the place where they come from, but they shoot them and dump them into the gutter.”

I crossed myself.

“They call it ‘sacas’.” She added, picked up her washing and left.

I stood there, unable to move. My mind was wondering about the infamous ‘sacas’. When I went to see Mother, I didn’t say anything about the ‘sacas’. But she may have been told by her customers already.

Chapter 39

Weeks of hunger turned to months of despair: No news from anyone. One night a man came to my parent's house and told them were in a concentration camp near Cardona. At least we knew they were alive, but we didn't know for how long. The Ebro was a nightmare that followed me around night and day. I feared Marcel-lí might be dead in a mass grave.

Two months later, Oriól was allowed home. His body was a nest of lice, and he was so weak he hardly could stand on his feet. In the concentration camp, days went by without any food. In the mornings they were forced to sing the Falangist national anthem, but they had no voice left to sing. Then in the evening, they were fed a pot of watery lentils with pork fat. Then Ernest also came home in pretty much the same condition as Oriól.

Day by day and our life took a new turn: Oriól found work with the timber company where he had worked before the war. We moved to a village by the river Llobregat called El Pont. Our new house had a hole in the middle because a bomb had fallen in the corridor, but Oriól repaired it. On the river, there was a wooden bridge, and the fast mountain river flowing underneath. On the other side of the river, there was a station with a steam train carrying coal from some mines further up the hills to Barcelona. It also carried passengers in quaint, wooden carriages that moved sideways and shook as it travelled parallel to the meandering river. I used to wonder how it managed to stay on the rails and not fall into the water. When the train whistled, Nina and I laughed madly: it was as if the shrill sound of the whistle was calling us to wake up to a new life.

Between the crags, there was the church where our uncle was the priest before the militia killed him. Every time I looked at those peaks, I felt a terrible emptiness. Now that we were so near and we could visit him regularly; he wasn't there anymore.

There was a wooden footbridge leading to the main entrance door of our house; when I walked on it, the boards creaked, and I feared they might break. I would slip through the boards and fall into the gap. The cat didn't mind sleeping on the wooden bannister. When I looked at him, I saw fear in his bright eyes; he reminded me of Mother's house that was now too far to visit. We had to walk a few miles, although there was a connecting bus service, we had no money to pay for it.

Our Catalan Language was forbidden, and soon Nina spoke perfect Spanish. I wasn't able to associate certain words like Romani with the Castillian name Rosemary. It didn't have the same homely feeling. I imagined Rosemary to be a different plant that grew in a faraway place altogether. We plodded along in the muddled-up world of being forced to conform to the Fascist's ideas.

Nina was happy; she seemed to have forgotten the war. She made new friends and felt grown up because she was able to come back home with older children. Nina also discovered that her mum didn't understand the Castillian language. On her return from school in the afternoon, she played with the cat.

Oriól's employment consisted of supervising a timber warehouse just behind ours. Lorries loaded with pine tree trunks came to unload them, and then they were cut into smaller pieces. Having him home gave me some security. Nina loved to play with the piles of sawdust that collected under the mechanical saws. The feel of sawdust in my fingers gave me the shivers, and I avoided touching it, but Nina loved it.

After Oriól collected his first wages, he started to buy the Vanguardia newspaper hoping to see news about bullfighting. I couldn't understand that weird passion of his, but since we had food, it was better to keep my mouth shut.

Although the river Llobregat was a fast mountain river; near the house, it spread over a shallow bed of pebbles and left behind a continuous musical sound; but the water was black. I looked at that stretch of black water flowing down between river boulders and dislodged mountain rocks; I thought of a life going nowhere. I wondered whether all the rivers in the country had dirty water and asked Oriól.

"Further up the hills, there are coal mines and washing the coal makes the water black," he replied.

"But the river looks sad," I said.

"It's only dust sediments on the pebbles," he added.

"I miss the pool's clear reflections of the rivers in Llinas," I said.

"Yes, I also miss the summer days when I played by the sea," Oriól grinned.

"It's like the blackness of the night following me during the day," I said, getting irritated because he wasn't able to understand my feelings.

"Today it's a sunny Saturday."

"I feel cheated of the simple joys of life."

"Now it's time to think about work because Nina needs education."

Then, I realised that the religious education that Nina was going to have was not the education that he would have liked for her. Josep came to see us, his girlfriend lived halfway from the town, and our village and Mother had insisted that he should come. Franco's reign of terror was in full swing, and we were all terrified of the news. The ones passed by word of mouth.

"In the inn, I heard a man saying that in Franco's concentration camps the worse killer was a disease," I sat holding my head with my hands in the horror of the harrowing existence that Marcel-lí was going through.

"Would Marcel-lí survive?" I asked.

"Well, he went to fight as a volunteer, and I don't know," replied Josep.

"His uncle's a priest, and he may be able to help," said Oriol but I didn't believe him.

"But even if he survives the executions, he may not survive the illness. Remember his wound in the chest.

Chapter 40

1941 Rosana

Three years, past and one day, I glimpsed the cat scuttling away, the footbridge creaked, and I felt a strange feeling in my throat. "It's Marcel-lí," I said to myself and rushed out of the kitchen to open the door. He stood in front of me tall, thin and pale, but he was still handsome. I threw myself into his arms, and I felt as if we were both back up in the hills.

I eyed him from head to toe. His hair was short, his fleshy lips pink and his forehead broader. The dark and puffy rings under his eyes made him look older than his twenty-four. His eyes still retained an extraordinary look as if he was able to see far beyond our ordinary life. I took a deep breath and said.

"You've no idea how happy I am."

"I'm pleased to be here," he said.

"Come and see our new home," I pushed the door open.

With a long stride, he crossed the wooden step and came straight into the hall. With an elegant movement, he turned right around and looked at the bare walls.

"I feared I would never see you again," I said with a sigh.

"Well, I'm here."

I gave him a chair. He sat at the table and lit a cigarette. I got a bottle of red wine and a glass from the cupboard and put them on the table.

"Have a drink. You must be thirsty."

At that moment, the spot of sunlight that fell on the table disappeared. The cat had returned to the bannister, but the sun remained hidden.

"You must take care of yourself," I said, "to love your country is not the same thing as owning it," I said. Marcel-lí laughed.

Nina got back from school. She picked up the cat and came into the house stroking the cat lovingly. She stood in front of Marcel-lí holding her books and the cat in her arms.

"This is your uncle Marcel-lí," I said.

"The uncle who was in prison?" she asked and put the books on the table with her right hand and holding the cat with the left.

"Yes, I'm the one," he replied.

"Why?

"Because I didn't believe what they believed," he replied.

"Our teacher says that people who don't believe in God are bad, but my dad doesn't believe in God and he's a good man and he hasn't been in prison."

"It's more complicated than just believing in God or not. We fought to defend the right to believe or not to believe, and the Fascist didn't like it."

I served bread and dry sausage. Oriól got back from work, and Marcel-lí stood up.

"I saw you were coming to the house," Oriól said. "How are you?"

"Well, I've survived," Marcel-lí smiled, and they both shook hands and sat down.

"It's quite a surprise," Oriól said.

I left them alone and went to the kitchen to cook supper with Nina. I began to

peel the potatoes, and she washed the cabbage. She liked to do things properly.

"What're you going to do?" I heard Oriól asking.

"I'll try to find work on a farm but..."

"Difficult," Oriól said, "difficult and badly paid."

"Well it's life and, after what I've been through, I need to be close to living things."

"I've been in a concentration camp myself," Oriól replied, "I tasted the hunger, suffered dysentery, and felt the lice on my head." Marcel-lí nodded.

"In Albateras there were also executions. They would take place several times a week. We had to stand to attention in front of the camp's authorities: a commission of Falangist, a priest and the head of the local civil guard. The Falangists had come from all over the country to identify Republicans from their hometowns. " Marcel-lí hesitated, "Hunger and sickness had reduced every one of us to a bundle of shaking bones. I feared I might collapse. The Falangist called out a few names, ordered those men to stand forwards in front of an execution squad. We had to raise our right hand and sing the Falangist anthem 'Cara al Sol'. A metallic taste like rust filled my mouth:

gunshots, clouds of smoke, our friends fell straight onto the ground bleeding to death."

Oriól moved uncomfortably in his chair. The smell of streaky bacon I was frying made me feel sick, and Nina gave me a sad look.

"We also had a little fun, we found a piece of newspaper, and it said that Franco went to the church of Santa Barbara north of Madrid, and offered his sword to God as thanks for his victory." Oriól sighed and laughed nervously, but Marcel-lí laughed loudly, and in a frightening way.

"Why do Father and Uncle laugh like that?" Nina asked.

"It might be because they haven't seen each other since the beginning of the war."

I replied.

I didn't eat that night, but they enjoyed the mashed potatoes, cabbage and bacon. I sent Nina to bed, and Marcel-lí left the house late. Oriól closed the door and looked me in the face.

"Did you hear Marcel-lí? Did you see any of the compassion or forgiveness that the church preaches so much?

I shook my head.

"They are bastards!" Oriól shouted, and he went to bed.

Marcel-lí had to go back to prison to serve the rest of the 15 years of his sentence. He refused to go back and to keep a job was difficult: His employers were afraid of the Civil Guard. Mother found him jobs, but he had retreated further and further away from us.

Chapter 41

Spring 1942. In the Catalan hills

I was working in the hills in the north of Catalonia, cutting trees and clearing overgrown vegetation. It was all sweat and toil, but the war fugitives had killed the last wolves of the region, and the boar hunting season was over, I had a magnificent stretch of forest to myself. And the red pines had never smelled so fresh.

One evening, I took a break to get a splinter out of my finger when I spotted a group of armed men. At first, I was worried because I thought they were Civil Guards. But as they approached and I saw their hungry faces, ragged clothes, and sunken eyes, I had no doubt these men had just escaped one of Franco's prisons. The worn-out men told me that they had lost their way while trying to cross over the Pyrenees. They planned to set up camp in the south of France and from there make an incursion into Spanish territory and fight to overthrow the Fascist regime. World War 2 was ending, and that meant the

Allied forces were winning, so getting rid of Franco was becoming a possibility.

The escaped prisoners invited me to join them, but although I was very impressed by the men's courage at that point, I wasn't ready for the project. However, after a lot of pondering I thought out a similar plan if it was going to succeed, it was essential to learn the tracks that connect Catalonia with France: I would need a safe escape route. First, I joined a group of smugglers that trekked across to Andorra to buy cigarettes, French Cognac and other little luxuries that were a lot more expensive at home and could sell for a profit.

The most difficult would be to leave my family. The war had reduced my country to such an oppressive state that there was no room for me in my own house. A pack of mad dogs was persecuting me. I had to escape. Hopefully, Franco wouldn't be in power for long.

Rosana didn't want me to go. She was all tears. She said that if I went away, I wouldn't be able to come back and she won't see me again. Oriol understood my situation better, and I had the feeling that he was glad that I planned to go away. I didn't dare to go and say goodbye to Mother. I feared that she might convince me not to go.

I joined a group of local smugglers that crossed the Pyrenees to Andorra and came back loaded with American cigarettes, condoms, pornographic magazines and other things banned at home. When I felt confident that I had learned the right track, I moved to the town of Tarascón-sur-Ariège. The Ariège Mountains were a refuge for exiled Spanish people, Jews from Paris and runaways from the nearby Vernet concentration camp. They eked out a living foraging in the forest and local farmers allowed them to make charcoal from the evergreen oaks.

On my days off, I used to sit with other ex-combatants in a small coffee shop right on the river bank. On the other side of the river, there was a big rock with a round tower built over it. At the top of the tower, there was a big clock. We enjoyed a cup of good coffee, shared a few cigarettes and a little banter. But soon, the conversation ended cursing bloody Franco and hating Hitler who won the war for him.

Chapter 42

One Sunday afternoon, I sat outside the usual café by the river. On the other side, there was a hillock with a tall, round tower with a clock. My friend Boots and Paul used to join me for a coffee, and we spend the whole afternoon ranting about the war. Those mental images won't go away. Boots never told us his real name or the place he came from. He spoke in a countryside accent, was shy with words and often asked questions. I guessed he was illiterate. With uncoordinated movements, Pau stomped into the scene. He eyed Anaïs, who was wiping tables, waved his hands and with a strong Spanish accent, shouted.

"Café, si'l vous plait."

Boots laughed, Anaïs giggled and walked into the café. Pau sat down and glanced, suspiciously, at the clock's face in the round tower as if it were a one-eyed monster.

He had fought at Madrid, and after the war, he ended in Miranda del Ebro Concentration Camp. In that infamous camp, he suffered long periods of boredom, hunger and the lack of hygiene endemic in all concentration camps. But he managed to escape and trekked across the Pyrenees, alone, surviving on roots, leaves, and berries. He arrived at Tarascon suffering from malnutrition and dysentery. Refugees nursed him back to health but since then suffered from short episodes of paranoia: he heard the voices of the Civil Guard talking about him.

Pau was of medium size, his hair was dark and curly his eyes grey, and he wore a beret. In Miranda del Ebro he had been diagnosed as having degenerative inclinations, low intelligence and rebellious temperament. But I never saw any of that: what I discovered in him was a need for justice and freedom. Anaïs returned and carefully put Pau's coffee on the table.

"Mercí Beau-coup!" he said. And with graceful steps, Anaïs got back inside. Pau put a spoonful of sugar into his coffee and began to stir smelling its rich aroma. I lit a cigarette and left the pack on the table so that the rest to help themselves.

"Merci," Boots said, took a cigarette and left the packet in front of Pau. He lit his cigarette and took a few puffs one after the other, soon the smoke swirled around, wrapping us up in the smell of coffee and cigarettes. The sun was warm, the air crisp and the river was flowing fast over its bed of shingles. To our joy, the Americans had landed in Normandy. The region began to breathe a new peace. The highest mountain picks were still white and defiant. I couldn't ignore its call for justice.

"We're fine here, but at home, there's no freedom," I said, pointing at the Pyrenees.

"France will soon be free of Nazis," Boots added.

"Bastards," Pau swore spat on the floor.

"But on the other side of the mountains, the Franco reigns supreme," I said.

"He is systematically executing the prisoners and we're here enjoying the warm sun," Pau added.

"We've to do something," I said to see the group's reaction. Franco has no power over here, and I've been thinking about making a few incursions to the other side of the border to blow up the electricity pylons that supply electricity to the whole region and the city of Barcelona," I said.

"Right," Boots' clicked his fingers.

Pau laughed, choked on his cigarette and then coughed.

"But we need guns," Boots said, "proper guns."

We discussed how to protect our relatives from Franco's harrowing reprisals. We decided to follow Boot's example of not telling anyone the place come from, nor his real name made sense. From that moment Pau was called Owl, and I was Pancho, sadly my nickname didn't protect my relatives because everyone in Berga knew who I was. The local mountains were the perfect place to train. The CNT in Toulouse had fought against the Nazis and had guns.

On a day off we headed to Toulouse. I met Owl and Boots at Tarascon Station. Owl looked odd. His shock of black hair was gone, and a line of white skin circled his forehead. We boarded the small train, and soon it juddered its way out of the station. After a few bumps, we found ourselves out of town. A patch of trees in full blossom appeared then lush cornfields, and a reflection of our faces appeared and disappeared in the window. It felt like a holiday.

On arrival to Toulouse Owl began to look around suspiciously and rushed out of the train. I feared that he was going to spoil the day."

The CNT Centre was on a long narrow street between the Midi Canal and the Cimètiery De La Tierre-Cabade, not far from the station. Along the Midi Canal the sun felt hot Owl put on his beret and to my dismay began to talk to himself.

"Murderers," he shouted looking at some people on the other side of the canal

"Just shut up," I said.

"Be quiet, we're almost there," Boots added.

The CNT's door we read.

'Franco Assassin.' In black and red letters. Inside the hall was crowded with refugees, sitting at long tables.

"Franco's police are here," Owl snarled.

"Fuck, you're going to spoil the meeting," I said.

"I smell the rotten smell."

"Oh! Look who's here." Boots said.

At the main table, I saw a woman with a familiar face.

"Federica Montseny!" I said.

"Amassing!?" Owl added.

"Absolutely," Boots said.

"To have survived the Gestapo and Franco's secret police is a significant achievement," I said.

Federica wore a white blouse and a dark blazer. Her round face looked thinner with two deep lines streaming down from both sides of her mouth, but she wore the same thick, black-framed glasses. Federica was doing what she did best, talk, but she didn't speak from a high podium and a microphone as she did before the war in Madrid. Now she was another survivor like the rest of us.

"A woman has the right to terminate a pregnancy," she said.

What we need is guns, not abortions, I thought.

"We should've enough sense of individual responsibility as to do that what is imposed by dictators."

"Spies, spies," Owl said, looking around the hall.

"Love of liberty and human dignity are the basic elements of the Anarchist creed..."

Sometime passed Federica still talked and Owl won't stop the rhetoric.

A senior CNT member saved the day. He allowed us to use the office, and at last, we were able to have a conversation in private. The CNT supported our project, enthusiastically and offered to discuss with the CNT whether we could have proper guns, ammunition, and powerful explosives. On the train, we talked about our first incursion.

Two weeks passed, and I received a letter from the head of the CNT saying that more CNT members wanted to join our group, I was over the moon. The next meeting was going to be in a Toulouse café. The two more to arrive had long legs, muscular thighs and big, grey eyes with thin, brown hair that fell over his eyes. We gave him the nickname of Grasshopper. His friend was rather thickset with short brown hair, and we nicknamed him Bear.

It was surprising to see how quickly the group was growing, and before our first day of training in the local hills, we were six members. A member we called Strings because he was rather skinny and worked in a cotton factory. And then, there was Shepherd. We nicknamed him Shepherd because although he was young, the skin on his face was rough with tiny red veins surface at the top of his nose. He liked to carry a stick he had curved himself out of forked boxwood branch and said that before the war broke out, he had been a shepherd. At the end of the meeting, I was in good spirits. We agreed that the next Sunday we'll go up the local hill to do our first training session.

It was a sunny afternoon with a fresh mountain breeze perfect for climbing up the steep hill. Out of the blue, just before starting to walk another CNT member turned up. He had been running and was out of breath. He wasn't very tall, and he sported a well-trimmed moustache, his skin was white and his hands soft, and his wavy hair was combed back without a hair out of place. I thought he was too sophisticated to put up a good fight. I almost rejected him. I had no idea then that he had left behind a wife and a daughter to join our cause, and later he became one of the many victims of his passion for freedom. We named him Citizen.

We were all united by shared experiences: we had fought in the front and survived the horrors of the concentration camps, and we aimed to avenge our dead friends and get rid of the hated Franco and his Civil Guard. I saved as much money as I could, bought proper mountain equipment and walked up to Andorra retracing the paths that I had crossed as a smuggler till I was confident that I could lead the fighters to success.

Chapter 43

After doing intense training in the hills, the following summer when we felt ready to make our first incursion. Loaded with food and armed with guns and ammunition, we gathered outside Tarascon and waited till dark. We didn't want to stir the locals' suspicion. At ten o'clock, we started to walk. We moved briskly along the river Rônne. The riverbank smelled of summer grass, the crickets chirped, we rattled on about the war and felt like heroes again.

By midnight we scrambled uphill using goats' paths. We only stopped once to wash the sweat off our faces in the cold water of a brook and eat. Having recovered our strength, we continued walking but in silence. At 3 am, the air-cooled, the hills became calm, and the night was perfect. But it was a tuff slog trekking up those rocky hills. When we had finally reached the highest pass in Andorra, the first rays of sunlight shone over a forest of fir trees. We stopped to rest at a small inn in a village on the river Valira, ate a fucking good breakfast and slept comfortably and didn't wake up till late in the afternoon. We bought bread and dry pork fat, took a taxi to the other side of Andorra. In the night we crossed over into Catalan territory. We took out our guns and went downhill moving ahead through patches of rugged terrain and fording the river Segre. In the evening, the thick fog forced us to stop.

The next morning, we woke up with a clear view of the El Cadí Mountain Range. We walked a few hours more; the birds sang, and I felt at home. Simple was lagging and tripping over on loose stones, or surfacing roots we found in our way.

"Breakfast time, boys," I said, dropping my rucksack on the floor. Grasshopper sat on the ground, opened his rucksack and got out a cottage loaf. I took out a chunk of pork fat, and I began to slice it into thick pieces. Grasshopper cut the bread with a pocket knife while Boots picked up the bread crumbs falling on the ground and ate them. After breakfast, Owl got very anxious and began one of his rants about our plans.

"I've got a hunch that ..."

"If you didn't have a hunch you wouldn't be you," interrupted Shepherd cutting a small piece of the pork fat.

"Yea," Dark nodded.

"I've got the feeling that our plans may not..."

"We're fighters," I said. "We don't follow premonitions; we fight for freedom."

"But we shouldn't assume that the international powers are going to be on our side," Owl added.

"Shit, just shut up!" Grasshopper said,

We went quiet for a while, and after eating, we trekked for a few hours more. That day we slept with our boots on. I was the first to keep watch while the others slept under bushes.

We got up in the afternoon and carried on walking all night. It was early in the morning when we had reached the village of Espinalbet. Upon the hills, the air was fresh. It was the place where the wealthiest families from Berga escaped the sultry summer's heat. We sat at a distance high up had breakfast and watched the wealthy, faithful and well-dressed holidaymakers walking to church for the ten o'clock Mass.

I left Grasshopper, Shepherd, and Bear outside, and I went in with Boots and Owl. The priest had started Mass when he saw us retrieve a few steps and almost bumped into the altar boy. The congregation coughed their breath some turned back, saw Boots and Owl with machine guns blocking the exit, cringed and shrunk their shoulders with an expression of terror. I climbed the pulpit with firm steps, and the machine gun in my hands addressed the stunned congregation.

"Ladies and Gentlemen, it's a well-known fact that in the town some people are starving. So, could you please show some Christian generosity and put some money into the collection tray."

Everyone searched into their pockets, and Grasshopper passed the tray around the pews. Silence and then the clicking of coins falling on the collection tray. When the collection ended, Grasshopper emptied the money into his rucksack and went out. Then I thanked the congregation for their generosity and reassured them that the money was going to a good cause. I walked out of the church with a feeling of exhilaration as when you destroy an enemy target. I joined the group outside, and we scrambled uphill and trekked for a few hours. By the river, Llobregat, we stopped to drink, wash, eat, and we felt great. Then Boots counted the money. We had collected 2000 pesetas. It was a good day. We headed towards the remote hamlet of La Nou—a few more hours of trekking through raff terrain. The local farmers eked out a living from the poor soil and a few domestic animals. There wasn't a road connecting the area with the more prosperous market town of Berga. My brother Ernest lived there as a boy, and our uncle Damia had been a priest. We trudge up the steep and narrow footpath between the crags for a few hours more. A blister in my left foot was wearing me down badly. It was already evening when we come to an isolated farmhouse.

We hid the guns and explosives in a crevice, and as we came close to the house, we saw the farm chickens roaming around peacefully next were confronted by two dogs barking ferociously. The chickens ran fast in a helter-skelter into the bushes. A middle-aged couple came out of the house. The man had a subdued look, and he walked with a halt. The wife's grey jumper was threadbare at the elbows, after saying hello she began to shake a dish of corn. The scared chickens returned, but not all at once.

The farmer looked surprised, but he was friendly. I asked him if we could rest there for a few days, and he nodded in agreement. I gave him some cash, and the sight of money brought a harmless smile to his face. We took the heavy boots off and sat outside and enjoying the evening air. The wife locked the last chickens in a shed, she went indoors and soon smoke began to come out of the chimney.

That night we had the first cooked food in a few days. While relishing every small bite of pork sausage, the man told us that he had heard that Franco was coming to visit the city of Manresa.

"Fuck the bastard!" I yelled.

"Bloody fox," Shepherd added.

As the anger turned into pain, I glanced at my friends: Shepherd's eyelid ticked; Grasshopper's jaw bone trembled; Dark's face paled, and Strings dropped his fork. A shadow of pain went through Boot's face, and as the farmer looked more and more perplexed. Owl covered his face with both hands, got up and left without an apology. A strange silence followed; it was as if for a moment, we had ceased to breathe. Grasshopper was the first to move his hands, wiped his plate clean with the last crust of bread, drank more wine, lit a cigarette and also left. One by one, we followed suit and having found a comfortable patch of grass we sat to discuss possible ways to kill the hateful dictator. Having agreed on a plan, we went to bed and slept till late the next day.

In the evening we left the house and walked towards the line of electricity pylons that supply the industrial area of the river Llobregat and the city of Barcelona. We lay on a soft bed of pine needles, and at the first light of dawn, we planted two plastic tablets at the base of an electricity pylon, lit the fuse and ran to a safe distance. Within a few seconds, there was a powerful blast, and a cloud of dust followed by an explosion of shouting.

"Bravo! Bravo!"

Grasshopper jumped up and down and began to cough. And as the dust began to settle the broken pylon emerged with more screams, more cheers, and more coughs. I couldn't believe why such a small victory could be so great. It would take a long time before the authorities would find the electricity pylon, repair it and put it to work again.

We walked out of the area along through pine groves and scrubby hills for several hours. At dusk, we bumped into a boar that ran scared out of our way. Having reached a moonlit clearing, we sat to discuss our plan in detail. We would need to book a posh hotel with a good view of the High Street and cars to run away after the attack. We decided to steal the payroll money of the Cardona's Potassium Mines. I liked the idea because the company would pay its workers all the same: we were not going to steal from the poor. Having agreed on the plan, we left the low hills fast and walked all night till we found a resting place in an evergreen grove not far from the mines.

I relied on a school friend who lived in Cardona, and luckily, I still remembered his address. I went to see him, and he supported our plan with great enthusiasm. He would stand on a hill with a good view of the road, and as the Ford that carried the money approached, he would wave his beret. The group would split in two: Dark and I were going to stop the car holding our guns and demand the money. Having long legs, Grasshopper was going to take the money and run into the bushes; the rest of the group was going to cover in case we encountered some resistance.

On Saturday, we took our positions according to our plan, but there was no sight of my friend. A Ford passed by, but we were not sure whether it was the right one. Apart from not being completely black, the car was too new. A few drops of rain fell, and another car approached, that car was an old Ford with a small body and a big backside. That was probably the one, but we didn't want to risk it. Next, a farmer's cart was pulled by a horse and the farmer holding the holster passed, slowly and slowly in front of us. More rain then, a lorry loaded with waste from the mines.

"Fuck the bastard!" Grasshopper shouted. Dark lifted his gun as if threatening the sky. Owl covered his head with both hands and screamed, Shepherd began to swipe the grass with his stick, and I despaired. We may never have such an opportunity again. String looked beyond the hills in silence, and I wondered what was going on through his head. To come to terms with the missing top dog was not only painful, but it was also very humiliating. In the evening, the rain turned to a cold wind, and we retreated under a wet blanket back to the hills, cursing the dictator and our bad luck.

String decided to go to Barcelona and set up his resistance group. It was a real loss; he was an experienced fighter. He had fought on the Ebro front, survived the Almendros concentration camp and like the rest of the group crossed over to France. I had no faith in his project and tried hard to dissuade them from abandoning it. I told him that in the city there was no way to retreat and you could easily fall into a police gauntlet. But nothing I said could put him off his project.

Chapter 44

On our retreat back to France, we stopped in Santa Eugenia and had a properly cooked meal. At twilight we picked up our rucksacks with food, water and our weapons: you never knew what kind of danger was waiting for you. No one knew which path we were going to follow: there could be a Franco spy among the group, and we could meet the Civil Guard anywhere. At first, the tracks were narrow and slippery, but since we didn't carry any explosives, it was an easy downhill walk. In the village of Vilada, a faint moonlight allowed us a safe crossing of the River Llobregat.

From then on, we struggled uphill for a few hours, stopping only for short breaks. We ate and during the day slept under bushes, and when it was dark enough, we started to walk towards Pla de Erol. In the middle of the night, as we approached a forest of firs, the usual forest sounds went dead silent, the moonlight dimmed, and Shepherd shouted.

Collon, collons estem fotuts."

"No need to panic," I said, as a cloud of thick, powdery mist was falling over the forest. Shit, it was serious. We had eaten all the food, and if we didn't manage to cross the border before dawn, we'd have to spend one more day hiding in the forest chewing box leaves. We stumbled along with ghostly firs, trampling on turf or tripping on low branches amid a chorus of curses against Franco.

Having left behind the firs and pines, we were exhausted. A short rest by a stream and we continued through stretches of overgrazed land and bare ridges. Further up, I recognised the loud sound of the Torrent de Coll Marcer. We were in the right place.

As we trudged up the noisy torrent, the mist began to thin. We were able to quicken our pace. Just before dawn, we had managed to cross the River Villallovent on the border. At last! We had we were in France. We dropped the rucksacks and had a good rest. While walking to Ossejá, we spotted a farmhouse. An old man was opening the cows' shed. Seeing two cows squabbling over a patch of grass made me feel at home. We approached the man and asked if we could stay for a couple of days, and from that day on Mass Tartás became a regular stop after the future border crossing. The group split in half and scattered throughout the Rônne Valley.

In the Ariège, it was difficult to find work. The grape harvest was late that year, but the Ariège had no vineyards. At times, you could hear older men telling stories of the days when the region had a class of excellent white wine. However, after World War 1, local vineyards were uprooted to grow wheat.

Owl was lucky. He got a job on a local farm, harvesting Swedes and the evening. He cooked them in a big cauldron to feed them to farm animals. Boots had to go further up the river to seek work. I returned to Madame Bonheur's modest guest house, did some repairs for her and eventually, found a job at a building site. I spend my days carrying bricks, buckets of water and sacks of cement, and then mixing it all in a mortar trough. And among splashes of mortar, jokes, and swearing, it was nice to see a neat, brick wall getting higher every day.

I woke up to the rattling of an empty tin rolling down the street. I cursed the bloody win. The Ariège is a windy place Madame Bonheur used to say. She didn't like her guests swearing in her modest house. So, I walked to the toilet cursing in a low voice like an upper-class lady. Madame used the pages of glossy magazines to hide the crumbling paint on the wall, and I sat there looking at the magnetic smile of Rita Hayward in front of me. She had a unique talent for combining beautiful faces with flowery spring landscapes. Out in the corridor, I bumped into her as she was rushing around closing the shutters.

"Oh, la la! It's the Black Mistral!" she said. "It brings bad luck."

The wind kept me out of work, and there I was in bed all morning wrapped up in blankets in the darkroom. Outside, the horrid wind was tearing the branches of the ash trees. My mind was sinking into the past. Another crack and another branch collapsing like a dead body with all the limbs stretched out on the ground. I saw my dead friends coming alive. We were in Quinto at the beginning of the war. I could hear the rattling of the machine gun. Then they appeared again, but this time we were in the concentration camp lying in a pool of blood. I jumped out of bed and rushed out to the street. Another gust of wind, a cloud of dust billowed along clouding my eyes, leaves flew above the trees and awnings rattled, and hinges creaked furiously.

In the riverside café, I had a surprise: Owl was there sitting on his own, his face hidden behind the recently published Le Monde newspaper, not far from a few men involved in a noisy card game. Empty cups lay on the tables, and the floor was strewn with flimsy paper serviettes.

I approached the bar, and this time I ordered a glass of Pinot Noir and sat next to Owl.

"Hey, man! No work for you today?"

"Oh, I'll clean the sty later," he said, waving his right hand.

"What a mess," I said.

"Anaïs didn't come to work," he added.

My wine arrived. I sipped the rich wine left the glass on the table and picked up the paper. I riffled through the pages. I skipped Picasso's Bull Head that caused so much stir everywhere. I read that the Germans had retreated from Greece.

"Great! The war will soon be over." I no longer cared about the outside wind.

"We ought to plan another incursion," I said.

"Yeah, but blowing electricity pylons alone won't go far."

"We've to do something, even if it's only to keep the madness at bay."

"We need the help of the international community otherwise we'll never recover our country."

But I felt compelled to do something. Trekking across the mountains was freedom; the only freedom I knew.

At the end of March, the warm White Mistral had dried the stagnant water and had swept away all winter clouds. The sky was now clear, beyond mount Vetdessos, the snow-white Pyrenees stood there like a call to achieve something great: Freedom. The cause was worth the struggle and seeing the farmers sowing sunflower seeds. I decided it was time to organise another incursion. This time we met in a Toulouse coffee shop.

Most members turned up, and as the last packets of Gauloisse cigarettes lay empty on the table, we had organised a detailed plan. This time we were going to target the most prosperous cotton mill on the Llobregat River: the Colonia Rosal. The owners enjoyed a life of idle luxury in the city of Barcelona. Meanwhile, the workers laboured all day for a little money.

Chapter 45

Spring 1944

In the spring, I moved to Toulouse; I got a job in a building site; I wanted to be near the CNT and get the latest information about Spain. The first news I got was that Strings had been arrested, tortured and condemned to twenty years in jail. I was devastated; we had lost a real Maqui, a good fighter and an excellent friend. It took me some time to get used to a new job and life in the city. Then, in the CNT, I met María. She was a small, graceful woman in a blue dress. She stood chatting with two female friends. What attracted me most was not her black hair falling in waves over her soft face, but the courage in her poise: her feminine body reminded me of my foster Mother. I approached the group; they dispersed. Maria smiled.

"Hello, are you a refugee?" she said in a Barcelona accent. I laughed.

"A secret spy!"

She laughed at my country accent.

"I like the way you laugh," I said.

"Oh! It's the way you move your head."

I wasn't going to blurt out that I was a Maqui.

From that day on, María and I saw each other frequently, mostly in the CNT centre and sometimes we took a walk in the Gardin des Plants. I Maria was a true Marieanne: the statue symbolising the French Republic. I used to think that for her laugher was a form of revenge and she laughed at every trifle. Having lost her partner in the war and had to flee from possible execution or to have her head shaved and paraded through the city's street as a traitor. In Toulouse, she worked as a cleaner, and she was free to make fun of the church, the fascist authorities and the rich landlords who had propped up the fascist.

"Wait for the chickens to come home to roost," she would say and then, laughed. Laughter is healing, and together we made fun of the Spanish authorities wearing the same old clothes made with new materials, Mrs, Franco doing a cut walk with her stolen pearls. But one day we stopped laughing and began to speak in whispers. Love was more fun than laughter.

June turned out to be a month like no other: The Allies landed on Omaha Beach, Normandy. At the beginning of August, more troops landed on the Côte d'Azur, Provence. The Nazis decamped, hopped on their trucks and retreated up the Rônne Valley. towards the border with Germany. Ironically, the Nazis who had no time to escape were arrested and sent to Vernet Concentration Camp.

In the middle of august Paris was liberated: At last! Soon France would be free of Nazis. However, freedom had stopped at our country's door. It was time to act; we believed then that the world would help us to get rid of Franco's murderous regime.

The world was crying for justice, and the International scene was changing fast. We made another incursion, blew a few more pylons in the hope that to remind the self-appointed Generalisimo that there were people who were still ready to risk their lives for freedom.

A young man joined the group. He very was strong. I remember his healthy hair combed back. His forehead was broad, and his big, dark eyes were overflowing with humanity. I should have rejected him; he was far too young to become a victim to the course of freedom. In those days, we firmly believed that ideology was more important than life itself. The General Assembly of the United Nations in Los Angeles condemned Franco as a war criminal. And we were convinced then that we were on the right path to freedom.

Chapter 45

In the village of El Pont, a bad spirit must've been working against me that day because, in the morning, I tripped on an espadrille's lace and spilt half a glass of milk. I almost cried. Later while walking up the hill to collect Nina from school, I stepped on a dog's shit. It didn't matter how many times I wiped my espadrille on the grass the nasty smell followed me all the way home like an invisible presence. I slung my espadrilles into the river, but my frustration stayed with me for the rest of the day. I couldn't concentrate on my sewing; my fingers pushed the needle forwards while my mind flew back into the hills.

After our evening meal, I cleared the table and Nina sat doing homework. Oriól moved by the wood stove and leafed through the pages of the newspaper. He wanted to see how skillfully the bulls died. While doing the dishes, I remembered that Josep had not visited us for some time. Josep had not visited for a while. I wanted to know how Marcel-lí was getting on with his exploits.

"You ought to distance yourself from this man," Oriól replied with his eyes fixed on the paper.

"Well, you didn't grow up with him," I said.

"He's nothing but trouble."

"We haven't been to Mother's for a long time, we could go next Sunday," I added.

"Yes, let's go to see grandma," Nina said, lifting her pen from her notebook as if asking permission to speak.

"The walk is too long for you," Oriól added.

"But I want to play with the kittens."

"It would be fine; she can have a nap at Mother's," I said.

Oriól lifted his eyes from the paper, took a deep breath and added.

"I'm fine here, but if you want to go well, just go."

I decided to go. It was the first time in my married life that I did something out of my own will.

The following Sunday, I dressed Nina in her best pink dress, a white woolly jacket, and new espadrilles. After Mass, we left the usual gathering of distressed villagers talking about food vouchers, or disappeared relatives. At first, it was all uphill, and one bend followed another, and it seemed that we were getting nowhere. But as we reached a patch of bare soil, the sun glinted on small pieces of glass. It was the first time Nina saw it, and she thought it was pure magic.

As we passed by the Cockerel Farmhouse, hungry dogs barked wildly, and Nina got frightened. The rest of the walk was leisurely pace down the winding road to Berga. Being on the foothill, it was all uphill and downhill. We walked up some low bending steps and then another bend, and we found ourselves in the main square.

In the high street, well-dressed people strolled up and down and stopped to look at the shops.

"Mum! Have you seen that doll?" Nina said.

"Yes, it must cost a fortune."

"The eyes shine like blue glass,"

"And her dress is pink like yours," I said.

"I wonder who has money to buy such a doll," I said.

We left the doll with rich golden ringlets, and a lace petticoat and Nina saw the pictures of a beautiful blond actress.

"Where is this place? Nina asked gapping.

"It's a cinema."

"Can I go to the cinema?"

"Not now, we have no money and besides some films are not good for children."

More titillating than the cinema were the iced cakes in the shop window. We saw a display of pretty cakes decorated with yellow roses and green leaves. I had no idea how the pastry cook could do it. We went in and bought a small pastry called coca. It was all covered in sugar and pine kernels.

"Yummy, yummy," Nina mumbled, liking the sugar of her fingers.

So far, the day was all fun. But on reaching a neat row of small, cypress trees, I felt danger. Behind the trees, there was the Military Barracks. Two soldiers in big boots and muck-green uniforms stood in a perfect pose with crossed bayonets in front of a flight of stairs leading down the barracks large compound.

"Why do soldiers have guns?" Nina asked.

"To guard the main entrance," I replied.

"But why do they have to guard the entrance?"

"Oh, well...It must be something to do with the army."

One of the soldiers looked at me, and the memories of moors bayoneting innocent women flashed through my mind like a violent storm. I tried to quicken my pace and get away from there, but Nina was tired.

Further down, we left the main road, and we stopped at the cattle trough to drink water from a fountain and had a rest. The row of plane trees was showing their first buds, but the dirt road was strewn with mules' dung because that was the way army mules walked on their way to feed on the Noet's hill. We zigzagged our way to avoid potholes and puddles of mud. It was lunchtime when we arrived in the village. I was surprised to find an empty square. Mother was in the alleyway with a bucket of water.

"Oh! That's a surprise," Mother said and gave Nina a big kiss.

"We had coca with pine kernels," Nina said.

"Good, but you must be tired," Good Mother added.

"I'm not tired!" Nina replied.

Father and Ernest were sitting at the table. After kissing them, Nina disappeared searching for newborn kittens.

"She won't find any," Father said. "No food, so I killed them."

"Don't tell her," she walked all the way thinking of the kittens," I said.

Ernest had another drink of wine from the porró, wiped a drop of wine from his chin and said.

"Food rationing is the fascist legacy,"

The red patch on Mother's forehead looked raw, and her face got thinner.

"Mother, you do look a bit tired," I said.

"Marcel-lí's situation is driving her crazy," Father replied, "The boy has now joined a group of smugglers."

"He couldn't find a decent job," Ernest said.

"He's had a terrible time all those years in Solsona and then in the war. And after that prison with nothing to eat, anyone would go mad," Mother replied.

"Wake up Filomena, smuggling is a delinquent activity, and it's not his fault."

"His uncles are responsible for his rebellious behaviour," Mother said.

"If he had listened to me, he wouldn't be in this situation," Father added.

"We didn't think that the war could end this badly," Ernest said.

"A war is a war. In the beginning, everything is clear, but then it gets confused, and at the end, soldiers swap sides and the good and the bad blend together. The winning side thinks that God is on their side and so they think they have the right to do anything they like."

Father's face was tense, and as he spoke. He got up and went down to feed the cows. Nina returned with no kittens and a disappointed look on her face. Mother gave us bread and cheese, and after eating, we went to bed for an afternoon nap. We heard the sound of retreat. I decided it was time to get back.

Ernest came with us when we reached the city's main crossroads. We met a woman walking down towards us, looking very distressed.

"Don't go to St John's Square," she said "a man has dropped dead. An ambulance is taking him to the hospital."

"Thank you for your warning," Ernest crossed himself. We took a side road and did not stop because it was getting late. Halfway up the hill, Ernest said goodbye and turned back. I didn't expect Oriól to come to meet us, but he did. We found him further up near the village. We arrived home late, and Nina was too tired to eat supper and went straight to bed.

At daybreak the next morning there was a knock on the door.

"It must be the Civil Guard looking for Marcel-lí," I said.

Oriól put on his trousers and shouted.

"I'm coming."

"Good God! What're you doing here," I heard Oriól say.

I rushed to see for myself who had come so early. I saw Ernest collapsing on a chair.

"Josep is dead," he sobbed.

"What?"

"Josep died. He was the man that collapsed yesterday in St John's Square."

After the first shock, Ernest and I walked down the same road that I had walked the day before, but it didn't feel as if it was the same road. The sun shone, but it was a painful road. It was full of memories, regrets and all kinds of questions.

"How would I cope with such a loss?"

The neat rows of niches in the cemetery looked like hungry mouths eager to eat human flesh. At Mother's house, we cried more and between sobs and with the help of our neighbours we dyed our clothes. In the evening, they were still wet, and we dried them by the fire while we said the rosary.

It was too early for spring flowers, and sadly, Josep had only a simple wreath of coltsfoot with a red, silky ribbon streaming over both sides of his coffin. I dragged myself behind the coffin feeling, dead myself, all the way to the cemetery. Mother was too ill to come. There were so many young people at the ceremony. Since I didn't know them, I assumed they were friends of Josep from the dance hall. Despair tinged the morning.

The next day Mother tidied up Josep's belongings into the box that contained our dead uncle's clothes and added more mothballs. I went to town to sell the milk for her. As I passed St John's Square, I saw him sitting in the coffee bar, his neat hair parting stood out among his friends, but the vision faded as soon as I approached his chair.

Ernest went to work at the inn, doing what Josep had done before him. Ramón had a job in a local cotton mill. As I walked back home a few days later, the city's cemetery, reminded me of the unfortunate Josep dead and alone, with his dream of freedom and the tango buried with him. Further up the hill, I imagined Mother walking from the fields carrying a load of forage under her arm crying in the dark house, cooking for Father, feeding the cows; sustaining life the only way she knew.

Even though Nina was so delighted when I arrived back home, I felt a desperate need to close my eyes and forget, forget. In the evening, the sun sank, the moon was a thin crescent, and the river gorge was filling with mist; the air was stifling, and everything seemed to be disappearing. In my sleep, I walked down to the cemetery again; the rusty gate shrieked as I pushed it open. There was no moon, and I could see the graveyard was overgrown, and black water oozed out from the lichen-spotted tombstones; a bat screeched as it flapped around and settled in a cypress tree. I lay exhausted on the side by a heap of faded flowers. The air was damp and smelled of rotting wood. After a while, Josep appeared silently and lay on top of my body. I felt a mad desire to hold him and keep him inside myself; give him new life, but instead of his throbbing heart, I felt only an immense emptiness coming into my veins and taking over my life. I was suffocating. I stopped breathing.

"What a scream!"

Oriól was standing at the bedside.

"What's going on?"

I couldn't say anything.

"You're screaming. It was as if you had fallen into hell."

I only cried because I couldn't tell Oriól about my crazy nightmare. I felt guilty and dirty; I had violated Josep's memory. I would have to carry my guilt like a crossover on my shoulders because I had no intentions of confessing it to the priest. I only prayed to the Virgin Mary for forgiveness.

Chapter 46

It was already August when the group had saved enough money for the next project. After cleaning our guns and greasing our boots, the day arrived to start the trek. We trudge up the steep hill loaded with explosives, cursing the bloody fascist and puffing up like army mules. Having reached the hilltop, we had breakfast and a good sleep in the guest house. In the evening, we emerged fresh, relaxed and ready to enter Catalan territory. As before, we waited in the bushes until it was dark to cross the border. In Catalan country, we assembled the guns and kept our boots on. Going downhill provided some ease until we had to ford the river Segre. We walked along the Cadí Mountain range. It took three nights of trekking until we had reached Santa Eugenia.

Saturday, at ten o'clock in the morning a Ford Woody van stopped in front of the mill's office and delivered the payroll money. On the other side stood the Church of Sant Antoni and further up, there was a wall and a flight of steps leading to a block of workers' tenement. At the end of the passage, there was a tall, dark block with small windows. It was the convent of the Sisters of the Sacred Heart. On the ground floor, there was a girls' school, and behind the grim building, there was a canal harnessing the river's current into a large water wheel that generated the mill's energy.

Beyond the canal and the river, the jagged mountains stretched as far as France.

The next day, I washed, shaved and walked down to the town of Berga. I bought second-hand clothes, and I went to the local bar in St John's Square hoping to meet my old friends. Bad luck, instead there was a civil guard dressed in uniform.

"I'm here to kill that Massana." He said, fumbling in his pocket for his lighter. I approached him and lit his cigarette.

"Welcome to Berga," I said. I enjoyed coffee laced with cognac. Before I returned to our base in the mountains paid his bill, and I told the barman to inform the Civil Guard that it was Massana himself who paid for his coffee.

In Santa St Eugenia, the next morning when was still dark, we dug our stash of weapons and walked down to the Colonia Rosal and waited in the local bushes. At about ten o'clock, Dark went into the janitor's office to make inquiries about work. Shepherd waited outside the gate in case Dark got into difficulties and Grasshopper went inside the church ready for action. By ten o'clock I was smoking a cigarette and walking up and down. Through the factory's shaky windows, I could see rows of looms working with mechanical speed and perfect precision. As soon as the loom stopped, the weaver rushed to knot the broken thread, and the loom worked again. Shit, two girls approached and I worried that their presence was going to spoil the plan. I stared at them. They laughed and luckily walked away.

The van arrived. I threw my cigarette and retraced my steps. Grasshopper came out of the church, and the van's door opened. I took my gun and pointed it at the driver's head.

"Quick, hand me the money!" I screamed. He gave me the case. I grabbed it and passed it to Grasshopper. He ran towards the convent as I covered his exit with my gun and followed him.

Behind the convent, an old nun was hanging out the washing. In the canal, we met the rest of the group except Bear and Shepherd; they scrambled up the river gorge. That way, the Civil Guard won't know which way to go. When Dark and Shepherd arrived, we rested for a while walked fast and we reached the Pedret's stone bridge.

We plodded uphill for several hours till we reached Santa Eugenia farmhouse. Hid the weapons and the farmer's wife cooked some food, and we rested there for a few hours. We paid them well because those hill farms had to survive on very little. At dark, I walked back to our base, and the next day we blew a few more electricity pylons and returned to France.

In the Ariège, it was difficult to find work. The grape harvest was late that year, but the Ariège had no vineyards. At times, you could hear older men telling stories of the days when the region had a class of excellent white wine. However, after World War 1, local vineyards were uprooted to grow wheat.

Owl was lucky; he got a job on a local farm, harvesting swedes, and in the evening, he cooked them in a big cauldron to feed them to farm animals. Boots had to go further up the river to seek work. I returned to Madame Bonheur's modest guest house and did some repairs for her. Eventually, I also found a job at a building site. I spend my days carrying bricks, buckets of water and sacks of cement. Then I mixed the cement with the water in a mortar trough. And among splashes of mortar, jokes, and swearing, a brick wall was getting higher every day.

Chapter 47

Ariège is a windy place. One morning I woke up to the rattling of an empty tin rolling down the street.

"Fuck the wind," I mumbled: Madame Bonheur didn't like swearing in her house. I got up and went to the toilet, and I sat there looking at the magnetic smile of Rita Hayward in front of me. Madame used the pages of glossy magazines to conceal the crumbling paint on the wall. She had a unique talent for combining beautiful faces with flowery spring landscapes. Out in the corridor, I bumped into her as she was rushing around closing the shutters.

"Oh, la la! It's the Black Mistral!" she said. "It brings bad luck."

Shit, we don't need any more of that I thought.

The wind kept me out of work, and there I was in bed all morning wrapped up in blankets in the darkroom. Outside, the horrid wind was tearing the branches of the ash trees. My mind was sinking into the past. Another crack and another branch collapsing like a dead body with all the limbs stretched out on the ground. I saw my dead friends coming alive. We were in Quinto at the beginning of the war. I could hear the rattling of the machine gun. Then they appeared again but this time in Albateras Concentration Camp. They were lying dead in a pool of blood. I jumped out of bed and rushed out to the street. With another gust of wind, a cloud of dust billowed along clouding my eyes, leaves flew above the trees awnings rattled, and hinges creaked furiously.

In the riverside café, I had a surprise: Owl was there sitting on his own, his face hidden behind the recently published Le Monde newspaper, not far from a few men involved in a noisy card game. Near the bar, there was a pile of cigarette ends and used flimsy paper serviettes.

I approached the bar, and this time I ordered a glass of Pinot Noir and sat next to Owl.

"Hey, man! No work for you today?"

"Oh, I'll clean the sty later," he said, waving his right hand.

"What a mess," I said.

"Anaïs didn't come to work," he added. Without her, this place is a mess.

I sipped the rich wine left the glass on the table and picked up the paper rifling through the pages. I skipped Picasso's Bull Head which caused so much stir everywhere. I read that the Nazis had retreated from Greece.

"Great! The war will soon be over." I no longer cared about the outside wind.

"We ought to plan another incursion," I said.

"Yeah, but blowing electricity pylons alone won't go far."

"We've to do something, even if it's only to keep the madness at bay."

"We need the help of the international community otherwise we'll never recover our country."

I had to fight for freedom until the end of my days.

Chapter 48

Spring 1944

June turned out to be a month like no other. A month so extraordinary that it was going to be remembered in the history of the free world: The Allies landed in Omaha Beach. For the rest of the month, France was on tenterhooks. Soon the Allies were near Paris., and we began to breathe freely. I could envisage a free Catalonia and the Allies would have a secure base from where to operate. However, I didn't realise then that the Americans had a different plan. First, they had to liberate thousands of POWs, who were about to die of disease and malnutrition in German prison camps. Franco's prisoners had to wait.

I was organizing another incursion across the Pyrenes when the first Allies' bombs fell over the coastal towns of Marseille and Lyon, the citizens had left their homes and sheltered in the local mountains. We also experienced a few sporadic air attacks aimed at destroying bridges. Soon the second landing took place in the Côte d'Azur. I was convinced then that freedom was knocking on our door.

The French resistance swiftly, got into action, sabotaging the electricity installations, and the telephone lines and blocking the main roads. After two days of intense fighting, Toulouse was free. The Germans decamped at full tilt, and set alight the German Consulate and the Gestapo Headquarters. Then they hopped on their trucks and scurried up the Rônne Valley. Nothing in life could be more uplifting than to free the inmates of Vernet Concentration Camp. The very sick ones went to hospitals, others back to Paris and the rest joined the resistance. It was time to celebrate, laugh, drink and dance in circles all night.

The Nazis who had no time to escape were arrested and imprisoned in Vernet concentration camp. In the same prison where a few days before the Germans had held Spanish refugees from the Durruti Column, anti-fascist intellectuals and unfortunate Jews waiting to die in Dachau. The refugees joined the French resistance, forcing the Nazis further up to the French-German frontier in the Vosges mountains. After the liberation of Paris, the German Army concentrated towards the west of France near Belgium. Soon France would be free of Nazis.

The General Assembly of the United Nations condemned Franco as a war criminal. The international scene was changing fast, and the world was crying for justice. It was time to act; we believed then that the world would help us to get rid of Franco's murderous regime. We felt we were on the right path to freedom. We made another incursion and blew a few more pylons in the hope that to remind the self-appointed Generalissimo that there were people who were still ready to risk their lives for freedom. We needed money, plenty of money.

In that operation, we kidnapped the son of an innkeeper. We never had any intention of causing the young man any harm. We had collected a substantial amount, enough to buy a considerable number of explosives, ammunition and provisions.

Chapter 49

In that trek, we only carried explosives for our big operation. We travelled along the Llobregat valley and left explosives hidden in caves. Before we got back to France, we kidnapped the son of an innkeeper. We never had any intention of causing the young man any harm. We only needed more cash.

On the Pyrenees, the only enemy was the bad weather; it could be too hot, freezing, windy or misty. On our return to France, we walked out of Santa Eugenia down to Vilada and up again towards el Pla de Erol. In the middle of the night, as

As we approached a forest of firs, the moonlight began to dim, the sounds of the forest faded and Shepherd shouted.

Collon, collons estem fotuts."

"No need to panic," I said, as a cloud of thick mist was falling over our heads.

But if we didn't manage to cross the border before dawn, we'd have to spend one day hiding in the forest. We plodded along with ghostly firs, trampling on turf or tripping on low branches amid a chorus of curses against Franco. Having left behind the first and tall pines, we were exhausted. A short rest by a stream and we continued through stretches of overgrazed land jumped over a stream, overcoming crags and bare ridges. Further up, I recognised the sound of the Torrent de Coll Marcer.

"We're in the right place boys!"

We trudged arduously up the noisy torrent. A few hours later, the mist began to clear. We quickened our pace, and before dawn, we had managed to cross the border with France. At last! We were safe. We dropped the rucksacks and lay on the soft grass. When the sun was out, we heard a cow's bell ringing we were near Ossejá. A farmhouse sat on a grassy hill, and the cows were grazing and fighting over a patch of grass. We approached the house, and we met an old man who came out to greet us. His name was Jules, and he lived alone. He allowed us to rest in the house for a few days.

Jules cooked lunch for us fried eggs, sausages tomatoes and bread and gave us the latest information. They told us that the allied forces had crossed the border with Belgium the fight was now In the Ardennes Germany. We rested a few days and helped him to do the hardest farm jobs, and Mas Tartás became a regular stop after the future border crossing. One by one, the group split in and scattered throughout the Rônne Valley seeking work. I went back to making mortar and laying bricks but for a different builder.

The Nazi army retreated further up to the frontier with Belgium and soon crossed the border into Germany. The dense Hùrtgen forest was a death trap for the Allied forces. The Germans had built bunkers, camouflaged among the vegetation and a wall that resembled a dragon's teeth to stop the advancing tanks. Late autumn rains and early winter snow bogged down the American Army. Moving war equipment in the snow was very difficult. The enemy could be hiding behind the next tree.

In the south of France, the black Mistral arrived. It blew from the Italian Alps down the Rhônne Valley bringing along snowy clouds, cold weather and bad luck. It made us tense anxious and subdued. At work, tools slipped from my numb fingers, I splashed water in the wrong place, my work was slow the builder cursed the weather and I swore like mad. The snow-white peaks were swallowed by clouds and cold winds. The local lakes froze and the vegetation was stiff with frost.

In the front, the Allied soldiers had to fight in the most atrocious conditions. It was all cold and pain for them and psychological torture for us. The south of France was busy executing the old Nazi murderers and their French collaborators.

At the end of March, the warm White Mistral had dried the stagnant water and had swept away all winter clouds. The sky was now clear, beyond Mount Vetdessos, the snow-white Pyrenees stood there like a call to achieve something great: Freedom. The cause was worth the struggle and seeing the farmers sowing sunflower seeds. I decided it was time to organise another incursion. This time we met in a Toulouse coffee shop.

Most members turned up, and as the last packets of Gauloisse cigarettes lay empty on the table, we had organised a detailed plan. This time we were going to target the most prosperous cotton mill on the Llobregat River: the Colonia Rosal. Its owners lived a life of luxury in the city of Barcelona. However, the workers laboured all day for a little money. The deep, craggy river gorge would be a perfect escape route. The civil guard wouldn't be able to chase us. Our enthusiasm was strong, the plan was complete, only needed some money.

Chapter 50

Years went by, and the Maqui exploits fascinated and amused the people of the Llobregat region. Local villagers saw those narratives as distractions from the ongoing executions that took place all over Spain. Sadly, for Mother and me, these stories were no laughing matter. Each story about Maqui's success sparked new anxiety and horrible nightmares.

In summer, the Maqui would find ways of getting money to subsidize the movement and pay for the defence of prisoners. At times, they kidnapped the rich for a ransom, or robbed vans carrying the cash for the local factories. He never stole from the workers or the poor. On the contrary, they paid the farmers who sheltered them very well, and that earned the reputation that the local Maqui stole from the rich and gave to the poor. All I knew was he was kind-hearted and generous. But we knew that Franco wasn't going to tolerate anyone challenging his authority. We feared that the movement would end in a tragedy for us all.

That Sunday afternoon, we visited my parents in the village of La Valldan. If it weren't for Nina, I would have burst into tears. It was heartbreaking to see Mother's eyes sinking so deep into their sockets and looking here and there aimlessly as if trying to find something or simply to forget. Ernest dropped the paper on the table and greeted us. Father sat in front of the fire with the poker in his hand. He was hitting a piece of firewood to shake off the ash. Mother kissed Nina, and Ernest pulled the chairs from the table for Oriól and me to sit.

"Have you heard the latest story?" Ernest asked.

"The radio never says anything about the Maqui," Oriól added.

"No, the Civil Guard won't acknowledge such a challenge, yet more pylons get blown up. His exploits echo through the whole region. In the coffee bars, when you mention Marcel-lí, everyone explodes into laughter."

Oriól nodded.

"He was a fearless child," Father replied.

"He's got real guts," Ernest added, moving his chair close to the fire.

"And arrogance," Oriól said.

"He's out of touch with reality," Father added.

"He went to the village of La Plana pretending to apply for a job," Ernest

continued. "The office clerk told him that it was the wrong time to apply because the company had enough workers. Marcel-lí insisted on seeing the director because he had a personal message for him. The director came into the office; Marcel-lí got out the gun from his jacket and demanded the money. The director handed out the case to Marcel-lí. Then, to everyone's surprise, he asked for his trousers," Ernest said.

"The trousers?" mother asked.

"Yes, the trousers," Ernest laughed. "And he took the director's trousers in his hand, and he went to the door, he handed the money to a group member. Then, he frog-marched the director, who was notorious for humiliating his female workers, at gunpoint to walk along the rows of working looms and laughing women."

I hadn't seen Ernest so happy for a long time, but Oriól shook his head and bit his lip.

He's mixed up," Father said.

Mother put a cottage loaf on the table. Nina came out of Josep's room, where she had been playing with the kittens.

"I want to help," she said. Mother gave her a plate with homemade cheese, and Nina brought it to the table.

"It's his uncle's fault," Mother replied, bursting into tears again.

"I've never seen such a wayward child," Father said, shaking his head.

"His uncles should be in prison," Mother said and wiped her tears.

Oriól looked at Nina, who was trying to cut the cheese. Two mewling kittens came from the corridor, and Mother picked them up and put them inside her apron.

"Let's take them back before they shit on the floor."

The black kitten's little face peeped out; he unfurled its tiny claws gripping the apron's edge. Mother went out of the hall, holding the apron with both hands, and Nina followed her. Then there was a loud thump on the door; Ernest got up and rushed to see who it was. We heard voices that we didn't understand.

"No, not here," Ernest said."

We heard strange and heavy footsteps coming up the creaky stairs. A scrawny civil guard appeared he was followed by a thickset one. Their cocky black, patent leather hats shone under the dirty light bulb. I felt as if death was lying in wait.

"We have orders to search this house," said the tall guard with a loud voice.

A bitter taste filled my mouth. I wanted to spit it out, but I couldn't move.

The big rifles in their hands made me squirm. Mother came out of Josep's room, holding Nina by her hand.

"God help us," Mother crossed herself. Nina hid behind her.

What if he's hiding in the loft? I thought to myself.

The tall guard began to search Father's bedroom, he opened the cupboard and looked under the bed. The young guard searched Mother's bedroom and ended up in Josep's.

"Stupid cat, let go," he shouted. We heard the kitten mewling. I imagined the kittens grabbing at his cape and the guard trying to pull it away. Nina rushed into the room to see the kittens. The tall guard got back, followed by Nina with the mewling kitten wrapped up in her skirt. The guard looked at the closed door leading to the loft.

"You open that door," he said, pointing a finger to Ernest. He opened the door, and they both disappeared up the shaky staircase.

"Turn over the hay," the guards.

I felt my knees give away, and I was afraid of falling. Father remained

Silent. Mother was trembling. Oriól held Nina, and she held the kitten close to her heart. The guards came down, and we began to breathe again. They stormed crossed the hall as their capes rustled and the floor heaved.

"Don't shelter him," the tall guard said. "It would have terrible consequences. They stomped down the stairs, the rusty hinges from the gate out outside creaked. We began to breathe. Oriól looked at Mother in the eye.

"He's been here then?" He asked.

"Only last night," Ernest added.

"For God sake keep out of this mess," Oriól shouted.

"He's my son," Mother said, wiping her tears with the apron.

"If he wants to die like a dog on the roadside; it's OK, but don't let him drag you along with him."

A death-like silence followed. I didn't feel well enough to walk back home; I wanted to stay with my parents, but Oriól had to go back to work. I went down to see him off, as he walked down, he said,

"This man is going to drive you all crazy. You and your Mother are too complacent. Marcel-lí's nothing but a crazy womaniser. When he's not chasing women, he's robbing people," Oriól shouted.

"He believes in what he's doing," I said.

"He's risking people's lives for a laugh."

In the evening after milking, Nina and I went with Mother to town to help sell the milk. Nina discovered for the first time that the town's oldest streets had little shrines with images of the Virgin Mary on its walls. Back at my parents' home, we all said the family rosary by the fire. Nina was tired and fell asleep halfway through, the way I used to when I was a little girl. We all slept in Mother's bed. I enjoyed the warmth and closeness of being at home again.

Chapter 51

The year 1945

After the cold and oppressive winter, the war ended in May with victory for the Allied forces. WW 2 had been the deadliest conflict humanity had ever seen. It left millions of refugees scattered all over the world, millions of dead and cities in ruins. Humanity demanded justice. Out of the chaos, a new order was emerging. Europe began to make social reforms: votes for women, free education, human rights, and welfare. And we believed then that Spain would be free like the rest of Europe. In December the European Charter of Human Rights was signed in Rome.

A good-looking young man wanted to join our group. I remember the straight hair combed back without a hair out of place, and the dark eyes overflowing with humanity. We nickname the enthusiastic young man, Simple. I should have rejected him; he was far too young to become a victim of Fascism. In those days, we firmly believed that without freedom, life was not worth living. We thought that we were on the right path that would lead our country to freedom.

The Maqui were committed to fighting till the end, some fighters left to fight in the cities. But I needed the freedom of the mountains I knew so well. If the Civil Guard were going to kill me, they would have to do a good run up steep hills to catch me.

At times, Maquis such as Captain Raymond would join us to perform certain operations. Like most of us, he had escaped from Franco's prison, crossed the Pyrenees and fought in the French resistance against the Nazi occupation. Well-known in France for his heroism Raymond never stopped his fight against Fascists till the end. But carrying explosives across the mountains was a very arduous enterprise. It required physical strength and faith in our cause.

The treacherous mountain weather was another enemy impossible to fight again,

had to endure. The worst experience I remember was one February. We had

planned to blow up a large number of electricity pylons, and we needed a good stash of

explosives. As far as Andorra, the weather was great but having crossed the border

to Catalonia it got freezing. We got under some thick bushes layered our

blankets together to preserve the warmth of our bodies and huddled up like a flock

of pigeons. The next morning, to our dismay, we saw the Cadí Mountain Range was

covered in snow. We were stuck, and since we didn't trust the farmhouses, we

found our way. We went clumping in the snow for two days without food. Having reached Santa Eugenia, we ate the most delicious casserole of hunter’s rice. After a

long rest, we walked as far as Manresa leaving the explosives well hidden in the

bushes for future operations and returning to France through a different route.

Chapter 52

I knew that one day, I would fall into action like the rest of those great men who dared to fight for freedom. Without freedom, we can't be ourselves, and life is not worth living. To deprive a man of his cultural and individual identity is a crime not only against his person but against humanity. Under occupation, people's only defence is the lie, and I couldn't live the life of a liar.

Our group had trekked through the Pyrenees for seven years and succeeded in sabotaging the electric system without problems. But near the border between France and Andorra, my fate took a different turn. Rainy weather forced us to change our route. We lost one day and had no food left. It was almost dark, and we had not yet crossed the border into Andorra. Boots I went to a local grocery store to buy the necessary provisions. The rest of the group was hiding nearby. Having paid the bill, the shopkeeper disappeared. I turned around ready to leave when I saw the flat hats of the border gendarmerie standing in front of us. The brigadier approached me and asked.

"Please open your rucksack?"

Boots dropped his rucksack on the floor; one of the gendarmes picked it up and turned it upside down.

"Bloody hell!" a few cartridges fell onto the floor. He had forgotten to leave his ammunition behind.

"What's this? The angry brigadier asked. He expected to find contraband a scatter of cartridges rolling on the floor.

"I need to see your documentation?"

I wasn't going to allow a border policeman to ruin our incursion. I got out my papers, and as he examined them, I pulled out my shotgun, pointed it at the brigadier's head and said.

"We're resistance fighters. We don't mean any harm. If you back off, we'll just leave."

At that moment, Owl and Grasshopper came to the scene with their shotguns in their hands. The brigadier tensed in defiance, but he put my papers in my papers my hand turned around and left. The rest followed suit. I put back the papers into my pocket. Boots picked up a few cartridges, and we grabbed our rucksacks and bolted. From time to time, I stole a glance to make sure no one was following us. Despite the rain, rushed up the steep hill like mules. The next morning, we reached Andorra, and there we rested all day.

As usual, we waited hidden in the bushes until we thought it was dark enough to make a secure border crossing into Catalonia. I didn't believe then, that the incident with the border Gendarmerie could have such an echo and I soon forgot all about it.

The trek to Catalonia was loaded with guns, and the explosives took much longer than the return trip. We trudged along in the darkness through patches of mud and long stretches of grass and ignored the few isolated farmhouses we found on our way. Having reached St Eugenia farmhouse, we were so exhausted that we needed to rest for two days.

Easy said he was homesick and wanted to join the Kiko group because they operated in the city. I saw the city like a spider's webs where no one could ever escape from them. I tried hard to explain to him that he was bound to be arrested, tortured and executed. But he had made up his mind and left.

Our first target was the Figuls coal mines. The following Saturday, we went into action. We had assaulted the car carrying the money before and didn't foresee any problems. At midmorning, we waited at a bend in the road for our lookout's signal. When we saw him waving on the hill, we prepared for action. But this time there were two cars. I assumed that the second car carried the money and the first the civil guards. As the vehicles slowed down, I jumped in front of the first, sending a wave of machine gunfire.

No one stirred. The driver was a local man, and I knew him.

"Fuck, what have you done? The man is the Doctor. I opened the door and saw the local Doctor pale and bleeding badly.

"Shit! I shot the wrong man."

There were no money bags and no civil guards.

"Sorry! Sorry!" I said.

"Get him to the hospital."

We scrambled up the hills empty-handed.

A few days later Francesc, the farmer in Santa Eugenia went to the village and on his return said that the Doctor was recovering in hospital, but our contact in the mines was arrested, tortured and killed.

"I won't stop till the bloody fox in a box," Citizen cursed.

We kept out of the town and in the farmhouse, Grasshopper made bread for us. My anger was building up, and I yelled at everyone beyond reason. Citizen had friends in Madrid, and he believed they would help him to kill Franco and also left. Owl's mind was busy fabricating stories about hearing the voices of the Civil Guard following our footsteps. Since we couldn't shut him up, walked up a wooded hillock and sat there watching the house. To our horror, a group of civil guards appeared and arrested the whole family. The sight of our friends being led away like animals was so painful that just I wanted to follow them and share their fate. More guards arrived, slaughtered the small farm animals and let the big ones down the hill.

Next three dead bodies appeared by the Vilada's bridge, and one was the farmer from Santa Eugenia. The following day the badly bruised bodies of two brothers from Sallent were also found dead in the gutter.

"Fuck! My brain nearly exploded; I knew the men were my uncles.

Bear had gone to the town, and he wasn't coming back. We feared the worst, and we dug up our store of explosives and buried them again in a different place and waited hidden in the thick vegetation till dark.

Chapter 53

In the village of El Pont like most people in the village, Nina and I walked up the hill to Mass. I was proud of my daughter dressed in her Sunday best, but I realised that her blue, cotton dress was already too short. Her white cardigan was still beautiful. Her curly had grown, and it was held back with a blue hairpin. At the church's entrance, we covered our heads with a veil and sat on a bench. The church was full of worshipers, the men still sat on the right and the women on the left. At the altar stood our Lady of the Roses with a ring of pink roses at her feet. The paint on the wall was cracking like the bark of an old oak. Nina was able to follow the Mass word by word with real devotion. The nuns at Amparo School had taught her the Mass in Latin.

The priest's sermon was about forgiveness and compassion, and each word echoed in the high ceiling. It felt empty of real meaning; in our world, I only saw revenge. I was ashamed of my ignorance and was ill at ease. There was a sickening smell of cheap perfume. It seemed that some women still had the money for such vain things as perfume. I was glad when the priest gave the final blessing. He strode back into the sacristy followed by the altar boys.

The congregation milled around by the small wicket gate, and one by one stepped out of the building. Outside, the sun was hot.

“Up in Alpens a man has been killed,” A farmer said.

My head spun, my limbs trembled, and I nearly fell.

"Is it Massana then?" A woman asked.

"Let's go," I said, pulling Nina away from the crowd.

"Mum, what happened?"

Overwhelming anger forced me to run away from the idle crowd.

"Let's get out of here," I said.

"Are they talking about Uncle Marcel-lí?"

"I don't know," I replied, tears welling up in my eyes.

We walked downhill fast for I feared what was going to happen next. At

Home Oriól was waiting for us.

“Why?" Nina asked.

“Who knows, they say an argument broke out between the farmworkers and the landlords. During the war, they left the area and, on their return, demanded the workers should pay them the due rent for the time they had been away. But the workers had no money. The landlords called the Civil Guard, and the guards ended the argument killing one of the workers. It had nothing to do with Maquis.”

Oriól switched the radio on and listened for more news. But we heard nothing about the crime.

A few days later three men had been found dead under the Vilada Bridge. No one had any doubts they had been executed by the Civil Guard. Two brothers appeared ad on a roadside, and we feared that more executions were coming ahead. Those days were full of horror and fear. The farmers in Alpens and a friend who was a visiting priest were murdered. No one knew who was responsible, but it was assumed that the cause was revenge. More Civil Guards showed up everywhere. They strutted around with their guns as if they were the rightful landlords of the country. They soon left, and the crimes were forgotten.

Chapter 54

That night we headed straight back to France but followed a different route. Owl's paranoia forced us to cross the river Llobregat through a different place. From the hill, we saw numerous civil guards waiting for us near the road. But we knew that they would never dare to infiltrate the thick vegetation: we had machine guns. We kept out of villages and farmhouses on our way. Just in case the Civil Guard were waiting for us. We trekked all night through pine groves, rocky outcrops and the odd stretch of grass.

The next day we rested under the bushes till twilight. Halfway back to France, a bank of rain clouds came from the East plunging the forest into darkness. Soon I didn't know where we were. We tried to quicken our pace, but our heavy limbs didn't respond. Red pine intermingled with bare birches. I sensed we were heading in the right direction. Monstrous rock faces appeared, and anger was turning to pain, my head was hot, and my body trembled. A peal of thunder rumbled, and I felt a drop of rain on my skin. Owl was the first to spot a ledge on a rock face, and we stumbled over a rocky slope until we reached a shallow cave.

"The ground feels soft," I said.

Boots lit his petrol lighter.

"Well, it's covered in goat's droppings," Owl added.

Boots dropped his rucksack and Owl began to jump to warm up his feet.

"I fear the local witches will keep us dancing all night," Boots said.

"I'm not in the mood for dancing," I replied. Grasshopper dropped his rucksack on the ground and went out. He got back dragging a branch of pine and began to break the small pieces. Another rumble, the earth shook, and water began to fall from the cave's ledge. Grasshopper crouched on the ground started to scrape the wet bark and made small pine cuttings.

"They're coming," Owl screamed.

"Shut up!" Boots said.

"I hear voices."

"Calm down," I said, "the civil guards are not going to chase us in this weather."

"You can be sure of that," Grasshopper added. He lit the pine cuttings, and we sat by the fire, warming up our hands over it. Pine resin bubbled, and Boots made a pile of dry goat's droppings and dropped them over the flames. They burned perfectly well, the smoke smelled like burning dry grass, and I felt at home—the cave's ceiling filled with smoke.

I walked outside to pee on the ground. I was floating in a sea of darkness, a flash of lightning flooded the forest in blue light, rain and more rain, the rain was washing the trees. A cold wind cooled my face, but my headache was getting worse as grief was turning to anger and anger to pain. My friends slept till the rain stopped. I watched the cave. After another night of walking, we would have reached La Collada de Tosas.

As the sun was rising the next morning, we had crossed the border, and we were safe in the country of freedom; because only those who have spent time in Franco's prison know what freedom is: liberty is feeling the air and sun on your tired skin. But luck my luck took a wrong turn. The next morning while keeping watch, I saw a black car approaching Mas Tartá. Shit! The Spanish Civil Guard is coming to arrest me. I took my short gun heading to the back of the house. I soon recognised Pascual, a CNT member.

"Bon día i benvingut a França! He said as came into the house.

"I came to get you out of here," he said and didn't wait for my unawareness. "You're in danger. While you're away, the French newspapers were full of stories about a Machi who had threatened a group of Border Gendarmerie and the French Police were searching the area to arrest you."

I had no choice: I had to follow him wherever we were going. Give me up to the French police and make peace with the country. I hugged my friends one by one as if it were the last time. I would never see them. I was worried about Owl, his mind was in such turmoil, during the day his eyes remain half-closed, his head bob and he walked around unsteadily. I wondered what was to become of the poor man. I just hoped that after a good rest, he would be able to return to his old job caring for pigs.

No choice, I had to follow Pascual advice and get the fuck out there quickly. As if more trouble was needed. Pascual added that Franco's Secret Services had hung posters everywhere, offering a hefty reward to anyone who could give any information about my whereabouts. As the saying goes: I was trapped like a rat; I knew that while I'll be serving a sentence for the possession of firearms and threatening the

Border Gendarmerie, Franco would grab the opportunity to claim my extradition.

I wanted to die in action on the Catalan Mountains, not in the hands of a bunch of Falangist war dogs. My main regret was leaving behind bloody Generalisimo safe in his solid throne of power well protected under a religious canopy. I was driven by car out of the Toulouse area. The road was bumpy, my head hot and was about to explode. The tortuous journey ended in a small village to hide in a friends' flat. I spend a few weeks closed in a void. Out of action, I was going mad. I had a double ear infection. My ached and idleness sapped all my energy. In the night I was unable to sleep and went to sleep came I dreamed about running to the top of the Pedra Forca mountain raging mad.

"Fascists idiots!" I screamed, "You can kill me, but you'll never kill our Catalan Culture!"

So much shouting and raging and mountain climbing, I woke up exhausted. As soon as I felt better, I reported to the police in Saint Girons. I spend a month in custody, and I had to pay a fine. I was freed on bail pending a hearing. I got a job in a quarry, and the work was hard, poorly paid and far from Saint Girons. I was forced to report to the police and had a terrible time.

On the day of the hearing, I had a big surprise: the Coflens Brigadier only accused me of carrying contraband. I was going to be free with only a fine. But I had to report to the local police. I got a job in a local quarry and lived in a barn. But worse of all was to witness the brutal exploitation of the workers. I told them to complain and then, the owners accused me of being a communist, and while walking along the streets with that label, I heard people mumbling. "Il e un communist." Villages would say as I passed on my way to the local shops. In that place, not only I was badly exploited, I was also ostracised, no one talk to me.

I left that hell and found a better-paid job in a coal mine. I managed to save some money and Maria came to see me and life was more bearable, but Franco missed no time to claim my extradition. I had to fight a different fight. This fight was a fight that I couldn't fight myself. Once again, I was in chains. I had to face another judgment, other accusations. The bureaucratic web was closing around me. Every day my mind was more entangled.

France had freedom and democracy; however, French workers had no voice. The country was falling into the hands of a bureaucratic élite who had no experience of ever having done a day's work. I feared this sticky bureaucracy more than death.

Josep Ester, a member of the CNT, who had survived Mauthausen concentration camp, rushed to my aid and worked tirelessly to achieve my freedom. Despite his support, my days were full of doubts, and every new day was ending with the same old uncertainties. At that time, I learned that Easy had been condemned to death. I was crushed. My body was exhausted with work, but my head was spinning like a mill going over and over the same question, how can I survive this ordeal?

The hearing took place in Toulouse's Court, as I was ushered into the courtroom my stomach turned; the court's stale air smelled of mildew like the Solsona

Cathedral. The well-ordered court's furniture stirred an old rage. I felt as if I were in the Cathedral again. Uncle's image flashed in my mind, ready to preach yet another sermon. I sat on the bench feeling robbed of my freedom, human rights and identity. The courtroom stirred into activity. In came the grey-suited public prosecutor with a pile of papers in his hand and ready to unload a litany of accusations.

I was accused of being a communist who stirred workers to rebellion: a degenerate bandit who for years he had terrorised local farmers; a triple murdered and a real danger to society. Merda, merda, merda! The word went around my mind. Therefore it was paramount that I was tried in the country where the alleged crimes had been committed.

The Judge listened with impressive serenity, calmly read Franco's letter and then, re-read it drop the letter on his desk, took a deep breath and said that my trial in the Spanish court had not been fair. Having fought for the Republic did not deserve fifteen years in prison. And about the accusation of a triple murder, he pointed out that Franco had not sent any evidence in support of his accusation and the case was dismissed. Franco's representatives nearly choked with rage, and I couldn't believe I was free. The prosecutor didn't move a finger; he was sure at the end of the day, he was going to get his pay.

It was time to think. I realised then that the law could be more effective than arm struggle. I decided to give up the armed struggle. But being the cunning fox that Franco was, I knew he would never give up. Stories appeared in the French and Spanish newspapers that I was a dangerous person. Every rape, murder and robbery that happened in Spain or France was blamed on the Maqui. Unfortunately, those stories were the only ones that the Spanish people were allowed to read.

In England, Churchill had been the first to recognise Franco. He said that Franco was a man of God, and thus, he abandoned Spain. Years of misery followed no jobs, no food, no freedom and prisoners were systematically executed in Franco's prisons. Europe was free of Nazism and Fascism, but Spain was sinking deeper and deeper into the middle ages.

The Toulouse CNT collected money to pay for Easy's defence, and luckily his death sentence was commuted to twenty years in prison. A feeling of relief came over me. I thought there would be peace, but there could never be any peace between Franco and me because he never gave up I was persecuted by Franco's spies and local newspapers made accusations that I was a danger to society. I had to leave the beautiful south and take refuge in the anonymity of a big city. Once again, Josep Ester was my saviour with his help. I was able to move to Paris. As soon as I found work as a mechanic, Maria joined me, and although anarchists didn't believe in the institution of marriage: we got married.

Chapter 54

A long time passed, I think it was more than a year, the spring sun was warm, and I had finished hanging out the washing. I threw the water that remained at the bottom of the bucket to geranium pots. The pink ones were beginning to open a few buds, but the red one was still closed. The postman approached the house, waving a letter in his hand.

"You've got a letter from Paris."

"From Paris?" I asked in disbelieve.

"Yes, look at the stamp,' he added, pointing at the corner of the letter.

"'Liberté, Frarnité. Egalité," his voice was so sweet that it echoed in my ear

like a forbidden love song. I picked up the letter and saw a blue stamp with a beautiful woman's face, but I only understood the word Liberté because the word is like in Catalan.' I thanked him and went indoors. I looked at the white envelope with the never seen before stamp and the back I read María and Paris. Paris was once the prison of Busar daying dream, so it must be a good place. I waited till evening when Oriól and Nina will be at home to read it. But when he arrived, I gave him the letter, and when he saw the French stamp, he said.

"We had enough of this Maqui."

With an angry jerk, Oriól threw it into the fire. Like a dead bird, the white envelope fell straight into the fire. Nina and I watched the envelope devoured by flames, the woman's face with those wonderful eyes and the word 'Liberté' turning into ashes.

"Finished," he said, and I saw the last bit of the envelope burning in the fireplace.

"Now the civil guard can come to search the house," Oriól said, rubbing his hands.

"They will find nothing."

"But I wanted to keep the stamp," Nina said, staring into the black fragments of what a moment ago had been a message from Marcel-lí.

"We mustn't keep anything that could implicate us with the Maqui."

I opened the door and went out of the house. I sat between my geraniums,

covered my face with my apron and cried. I remembered the time when Marcel-lí was brought to our house: the country was overwhelmed by a tide of grief. And he now left the country with no freedom and was devastated by grief.

Swallows also Fall

This essay deals with the joys and difficulties I encountered in trying to research and reconstruct the place and the lives of my grandparents, their children and their foster child Marcel-li Massana. The story deals with the period between1918-1951. 1918 is known as the year of the Spanish Flu. 1951, was the time when the resistance movement, known as the 'Maqui' was destroyed by Franco's civil Guard, and Massana was granted political asylum in Paris.

I never thought that reading a book could have changed the direction of my writing. But while reading 'Marcel-lí Massana L'home Més Buscat' by Josep Clara (Rafael, Dalmau, Barcelona, 2005), my book took a new turn; I decided to gather memories about my grandmother and the war. Sadly, a lot of information from that period had already been lost. The Spanish dictator General Franco ruled for a very long time, and people were afraid to talk about Massana. After Franco's death and by the time that Clara's well-researched biography of Massana was published, the people who had grown up with him, my father and my aunt, had already died. The first early years of Massana's life are entirely missing from Clara's book.

The first, supposedly nonfiction book that was written about Massana was by José Francisco is 'Conscience Speaks' (Ed. Acervo, Brazil 1966). The authorship of the book is unknown, and the book appears as if it is a 'confession' by Massana himself and other Maquis. It describes Massana and the other Maquis of the time as bandits and murderers who robbed and killed innocent people. Massana was described as living the life of a very rich man in France. The book was propaganda designed to discredit the resistance. To my surprise, when I visited Massana in Paris, he lived in a bedsit in the neighbourhood of Clamart. He worked as a mechanic, and his wife was a cleaner in a local school. Later, I read another factual biography written in Spanish, Marcelino Massana by Josep Maria Reguant. (Dopesa, Barcelona 1979) Reguant's account was much closer to the stories that my Father used to tell us. However, not a lot was mentioned about Massana's childhood in that book either.

Josep Clara is a Professor of History at the University of Barcelona, and his biography of the famous Maqui is meticulously well-researched, credible and consistent with our family's known history. However, as I previously mentioned, the first years of Massana's life are compressed into a single sentence. Massana's childhood is only an absence. I felt that the void had to be filled with some kind of human presence. I was the only person who knew about Massana's few years of childhood happiness that ended so abruptly and so painfully for him and for my family. My grandmother firmly believed that the strict religious upbringing to which he had been subjected to contributed to the kind of revolutionary man that Massana was from an early age.

The problem, in terms of memory recall, is that a long time has passed since those days. However, little by little, I was able to recall my grandmother's words. She would tell the tragedy of Massana's childhood to her family and friends. When I was a child, I would listen, but could not make sense of my grandmother's words, due to my innocence. My father also enjoyed telling funny anecdotes of Massana's exploits as leader of his group of Maquis. I began to see the story of Massana as something unique and worthy of further exploration.

I realised that I was in possession of personal information that could be woven into a meaningful story. I felt I was the only person who could write the book. However, all I possessed was a few fragments of a past and bits of information from books, internet research and my relatives, such as Nina and my older sister. She also remembers a few incomplete memories. I have added some content and cultural touches to give the story freshness and local colour, checking that all is consistent with the historic period.

The first thing I did was to visit my grandparents' village 'Castellar del Riu.' The village is comprised of three farmhouses all separated by considerable distances (about 1 or 2 kilometres) from each other. At the time of my visit, all the buildings were uninhabited. I could only find the landlord's house, and there was no one I could ask. On my second attempt, and with the help of a cousin who knew the area well, I discovered that my grandparents' house was a ramshackle building on the side of the large and imposing landlord's house.

I was thrilled to find that I was able to open the crumbling front door of my relatives' house, which had been closed from the outside and was only held by a piece of string. To my amazement, a way of life that had disappeared long ago reawakened in front of me. The old kitchen was at the entrance. It had been built on a dirt floor; the sink was the oldest that I had ever seen. It had been carved from a solid block of granite stone. Next, there was the cupboard that had star-shaped carvings on the door. That must have been the place where the cheese was left to ferment. At the centre, there was a corridor, and on the right, the hearth was enclosed by its round wall with an interior window to provide some light. I was overpowered by a feeling of exhilaration, similar to the emotion one feels while observing a great work of art.

I was immediately compelled to mentally resurrect the old place and give it life. I could imagine my grandmother's muscular fingers straining the milk curds and pushing them into the clay mould to make the cheese. I saw the whole family huddled together by the fire, saying the rosary. I imagined a bundle of lively flames rushing up the chimney. I could hear the sound of wood burning, crackling and breaking into separate glowing coals, as I had seen in my early life.

Then I followed the corridor and wandered through the rest of the house, while my cousin was calling me to come out because there was a danger that the building could collapse under the weight of my body. But I couldn't leave until I had seen each room. I imagined that the small room had been occupied by my aunt Rosana, the main narrator of the story. The house was on the edge of a steep hill, and the cold wind must have been able to penetrate the loose-fitting doors and windows and reach all corners of the place. In those days, the fire must have been the only luxury that life could offer to the poor inhabitants.

Since I knew the basic story, I thought it would be easy to write the book, which I believed could be finished in six months. I didn't realise then that simplicity can be both difficult to achieve and deceptive. The first problem I encountered was to place the story within a historical frame. I wanted the book to be written in a straightforward voice. Women were the passive victims of the war, and I chose to write the book in Rosana's voice because she was illiterate.

At the time of starting writing Nina, Rosana's daughter was the only surviving family member who could give some information. She only remembered the conflict as a kind of mist with a few surfacing bits of real life. At present, Nina is too depressed to want to talk about those days. However, she was able to recall in detail the dreadful day when the republican soldiers retreated and passed by the village's main road. She remembered, very clearly, the morning when the Italian planes bombed the trench on Noet's Hill, and the panic they suffered when fascist troops entered the village of La Valldan. Since the area was very religious, and no priest had been killed, the Moors were not allowed to rape or kill anyone.

In the nearby town of Gironella, the Moors stole everything they were able to carry. They seemed to have a special liking for watches. I remember overhearing the story about finding a dying young republican fighter near the farmhouse; the woman, who at the time, had lived in that house sounded upset even when she was telling the story twenty years later.

Back in London, I began to research the area using the internet. I rediscovered the beauty of those old mountains. I also realised that being close to France, those mountains and the whole area had seen the atrocities of wars with France and a lot of comings and goings across the border. This was the main reason why I decided to mention the French Busa Prison at the edge of the mountain range at the time of Napoleon's invasion of Spain.

Having researched the area, it was also necessary to research the Spanish Civil War; this was more difficult and emotionally painful. It stirred repressed memories of my father, Ernest, in the book. When the war broke out, he was in Zaragoza doing his military service. He was sent to Huesca to dig trenches and help evacuate the wounded. I remember him talking about the experience of risking his life to go out to defecate behind the bushes. I also remember how angry he was when he told us that the republican officer used to stand at the back of his troops with a pistol in his hand, threatening to kill any soldier who tried to escape. As a child, I had soon got bored with all that incomprehensible talk which to me, sounded odd, unreal and far away from the present time. I wanted my father to talk about the present, but the present was not happy either.

My family lived in my paternal grandparents' house in the village of La Valldan. Life was filled with arguments, new babies and little to eat. My father became ill with pleurisy, and we moved to live in a village with a cotton mill. Digging up those memories stirred a lot of repressed anger and sadness inside me; the injustices perpetrated by both sides during that war; the anger against the United States for the role they played and the subsequent international economic blockade. Anger and grief were my inheritance; anger provided me with the energy to work. Grief was the motivation to recreate the life of my grandmother and that of my aunt.

Quite often, I would spend a week researching battles, and only to realise that my story was not about battles. My story up to that point was only about how the women in my family had coped. So, I had to make my interpretations and fictionalise the gaps as authentically I could. The story about the neighbour Nuria, whose husband returned from the war only to die the next day, is real.

The information about the Ebro battle also came from the real experience of my uncle. He was at the Ebro and was a witness to atrocities like the opening of the floodgates of the Ebro's dams. This flooded the Ebro valley and drowned hundreds of Republican soldiers. Dead bodies littered the river bank and the surrounding countryside. The fascists sprayed the bodies with petrol and burnt them, or dumped them into the river, to stop the smell of rotting human flesh.

The destruction of the Basque town of Guernica is briefly mentioned in my book. It appears only as a nightmare, rather than a painful reality. A more detailed and harrowing account of the strafe bombing of the civil population by the German Condor Legion can be read in 'Spanish Front', Edited by Valentine Cunningham, p133, (Oxford University Press, 1986)

Alicante Harbour was another war horror from this period. I read Paul Preston meticulously well-written history of the war. 'The Spanish Holocaust', (Harper Press, p 479, 2012) According to him, refugees waited for three and a half days. Many committed suicides and the most vulnerable ones, such as babies and the elderly died. It became clear Franco didn't want peace; he wanted total victory and to exterminate the

Spanish Progressive Left. By then the international community had recognised Franco. Churchill said that Franco was a man of God. He was the first to acknowledge him. My interpretation of the harbour is a mixture of fiction and what I have read.

When I was a child, the small village of La Valldan was surrounded by fields and swallows were seen and heard everywhere. The songs and poetry of the time mentioned the swallows coming and going. Swallows were the first thing that appeared in my mind when I conceived the book. The birds are a symbol of the struggle of the local people. I wanted a simple plot and a naïve narrative voice, narrating the war from the point of view of simple village people. The swallows seemed to appear in the book almost by themselves. The fact that Hitler's planes, the Messerschmitt BF 109s were nicknamed swallows is a discovery that I made while researching the aviation involved in the war. However, it is not mentioned in the book because Rosana may not have known anything about warplanes.

The main difficulty encountered with the writing was in deciding which voices to use to narrate the story. The story had been conceived from the point of view of Rosana, I remember her as being very quiet and unassertive; she seemed as if nothing could alter her passivity. On the other hand, her mother, my grandmother, who had suffered brain damage later in life, could never stop talking. She talked day and night. I also thought that Marcel-lí's point of view was interesting and would be a contrast to Rosana's and would be needed to fill in the story where Rosana was not able to witness.

I saw my grandparents' family as a small country reflecting the political struggle of the time. Progressive Spanish people were strongly influenced by the liberal ideas that came from Paris and demanded social change. However, the wealthy landowners feared a French-style revolution and losing the money that they had accumulated during WW1. During that war, Spain had remained neutral. Young family members such as Josep and Marcel-lí embraced the progressive ideas of Anarchism, Feminisms and Darwinism. My grandfather was a staunch traditionalist. I remember him talking about the Carlist Wars. Those wars were the ruin of Spain and achieved nothing.

Reading several books on the war helped form long passages of information for the novel, but my supervisor pointed out that the writing was too condensed. I used too much reportage and I was rushing through material. The advice proved immensely useful: by demolishing the blocks of reportage style of writing, I was able to open new perspectives, add detail and emotional dimensions. I believe that my story is now more interesting in local detail and provides other people's views of the world beyond the immediate locale.

War survivors are still afraid of talking about the Maqui, even today. Painful memories had to be forgotten very quickly. The anger about the brutal repression of those days was expressed, scratching the plaster of old walls. The symbol of X appeared everywhere, where the wall was soft enough to be scratched with a pocket knife. The Catalan artist Antoni Tapiés, Victòria Combalia Dexeus (Ediciones Poligrafa, S.A.1984 p 37) found a lot of inspiration in those spontaneous scratchings of the letter X and the symbol of the cross. But his crosses are splashed with black paint, odd and imperfect. Tapiés takes the cross out of its religious context and uses it to express repressed anger and resistance.

I wanted to combine different elements of the story such as men's struggle for power and women's powerlessness, stoicism and resilience. Rosana is an example of the naivety of women in those days. Women were constantly criticised and forced to fit into the puritanical mould of the time. Rosana's untimely pregnancy before marriage was a stigma for the whole family. Tradition and family values were paramount. The concept of freedom and the needs of the individual were seen as mere whims that had to be ignored. Growing up was full of dangers; for a man, there was alcohol and prostitutes, for a woman, the possibility of getting pregnant.

Although so many years had passed, I have finally been able to make sense of what my grandmother was talking about in her broken sentences. Sadly, my story is only an echo of the pain and immense loss that the entire Catalan people were subjected to—first, the suppression of our language. Then, the imposition of a Spanish culture that was alien to the Catalan country. Catalan names were translated, and when a particular name did not exist in the Spanish language, they changed it to a name that sounded similar. This was a way of attacking our identity, denying our history and discrediting our country.

In conclusion, I don't think that the book is a complete work of fiction; it's not a work of social history either. I see my writing as an unfinished piece, a simple personal search or perhaps only a kind of mental process. An attempt at taking a glimpse from a window into the Spanish Civil war and then instead of staying longer and completing the story, I ran away from it because it's too painful for me to stay down in that nightmarish dungeon for too long.

Bibliography

Clara, Jospep, *Marcel-lí Massana, L'Home més Buscat* (Rafael Dalmau 2005)

Keene, Judith, *A mile to Huesca*, (New South Wales University Press1988)

Preston, Paul, the *Spanish Holocaust*, (Harper Press 2012)

Reguant, José María, *Marcelino Massana* (Ediciones Dopesa 1979)

MacDougall Ian *Voices from the Spanish Civil War*, (Polygon Edinburgh 1986)

Cunningham Valentine, *Spanish Front, Writers on the Civil War* (Oxford University Press 1986)

www.memoriahistorica.gob.es/Archivos. Accessed [November 2013]